THE FRAGMENTED SOUL

JACINTA MARTIN

CONTENTS

Beyond The Book Media, LLC

Alpharetta. GA

www.beyondthebookmedia.com

The publisher is not responsible for websites that are not owned by the publisher.

ISBN - 978-1-953788-00-9 (Printed)

To God
Thank you for waiting for me and removing the shame!

Decision Made

❧❧❧

Stumbling up the stairs to her dormitory, Naomi opened the heavy wooden door of her room. She crashed face-first into her bed with her purse still slung across her shoulder.

Thank God! was all Naomi could hear herself say in her head at that moment.

The night had been one blurry mixture of images filled with lots of dancing, drinking, and men who wanted her number. Naomi found herself enjoying the freedom that college life allowed but was starting to realize that if she kept this up, she might never finish school. Finally dozing off, she began to sleep away the excitement and drunken state she had so willingly participated.

Oh, my head!

What time is it?

Grabbing wildly around for her cell phone with her

eyes closed, Naomi finally found it. Reaching into her purse, which was attached to her, she grabbed her phone and saw the time read 5:00 AM. Getting only about three hours of sleep, Naomi awoke to her head pounding like a drummer in the middle of his drum solo. Glancing at her phone notifications, she was shocked to see seven text messages already from the men she gave her number.

I will read through those later.

Damn, my head hurts!

While lying in bed, Naomi tried to recall where she kept the bottle of aspirin because she knew once she moved, she would need to be quick. Too much movement, and she may not make it back to her bed. Suddenly she remembered the bottle was in her top dresser drawer, and her mini fridge that sat beside her bed was freshly stocked with water. Slowly sliding her legs to the side of the bed, Naomi finally steadied her feet onto the floor.

Using the railing on the edge of the bed, she gathered herself in an upright standing position. Moving slowly, Naomi made her way over toward the dresser, stood in front of it, and pulled out the aspirin bottle from the top drawer. Unscrewing the cap and tilting the bottle over, she counted out two pills as they rolled out. Popping them into her mouth, Naomi screwed the lid back on and tucked the bottle back into her top dresser drawer.

Holding onto the bed, she pivoted back toward the

head of the bed where the mini fridge sat. Bending over slightly, Naomi opened the door and pulled out a bottle of water. Twisting off the cap, she placed it to her lips and gulped down about half of it.

Well, I am thirsty!

What in the hell did I drink?

Realizing last night was probably too wild and that she needed more sleep to get rid of the person with the drum set to stop making noise, Naomi crept her way back on top of her bed. Closing her eyes and curling into a fetal position; she finally dozed off. The urge to pee awakened Naomi from what seemed like a cat nap. As she came to, she quickly realized the two aspirin pills from her dresser were not working fast enough.

I will just lay right here.

I don't have to go that bad.

She began to feel hot and knew she needed to get to the bathroom, but the pain in her head was too much to handle. As Naomi slowly braced herself to roll over and sit up, she heard something say get up and go to church.

Why would I do that?

I smell like whatever I drank last night; I need a shower, and my head is hurting badly.

Carefully making her way to the bathroom, she decided just to ignore the thought of going to the school chapel, church, or wherever.

Here Naomi was, in a position where she could barely move, and now she was supposed to think about what to wear, getting in the shower, and the long walk across campus; only to listen to someone preach. Under normal conditions, these things would have been straightforward tasks, but in the state she was in, they seemed like a daring feat.

As she exited the bathroom, the voice she heard earlier that said, "Get up and go to church" became even louder and more transparent than before. Realizing even in her drunken state, this was the voice of God; Naomi proceeded to give excuses for why she could not go and laid back down. It was not the first time God had spoken to her this way before. After resting for what seemed like another ten minutes, she heard God plead with her one last time, "Get up and go to church."

Rising from within Naomi was such a toxic mixture of anger, frustration, and disappointment that she had never expressed before. Her first year of college was nothing like she thought it would be. Naomi was excited to make friends with her roommate, but she was never around. There were many nights Naomi sat in bed alone a little homesick but did not want to admit it to her parents. Her teachers were strict, and her grades were not exactly where she wanted them to be. Naomi even thought about doing some creative things she enjoyed doing before but became intimidated by the number of people who were more creative than her. So, she didn't even bother to try. For Naomi, the feelings of inadequacy and comparison began to form and build as her first year progressed.

You will never be as talented as them.

Why would you want to do that?

You are just going to embarrass yourself.

Unable to contain the pain of those words, they finally began to bubble up and spilled out as she yelled uncontrollably in response to God, "No, I don't feel like going to church. I tried life your way, and this year did not produce anything but pain. I feel out of place here, and my expectations have been crushed. I don't want to follow your way anymore. I am DONE!" Naomi could not believe she had done that but felt she had jumped too far off the deep end to take those words back now.

After what seemed like a silence that lasted forever, she heard God say in the kindest, most gentle, and loving voice, "I will wait for you." Then the silence returned as Naomi laid her head back down on the pillow and fell fast asleep.

Naomi Mara Johnson had not always been like this. Growing up in California, Naomi thought she lived a beautiful life. Living in the suburbs, Naomi always thought life could get no better. Naomi's private school upbringing allowed her to experience things that she may not have been able to otherwise. Also, Naomi's mom, Linda, always made sure she and her sister, Lily, attended church regularly. Attendance included Friday or Saturday night children's choir rehearsal, sometimes sunrise service early Easter morning, and of course, Sunday morning services.

Linda also made sure that Naomi and Lily were readily available to volunteer for whatever the church needed a child to lead. Serving in the church did not bother Naomi as much because, from each of those experiences, she learned something different about herself. She realized she loved to sing, lead a bible study, and learn about who God said he was. Church for Naomi was where her relationship with God began. It was during her own time in her room listening to worship music and reading the Bible that He became more real.

She enjoyed getting to know who God was and how he cared for her, which she communicated by writing out her thoughts in her journals. The contents within each journal were everything from prayers, poems, stories, songs, things about her day, and so much more. It was through these interactions that her trust in God's ability to lead and speak to her developed.

For Naomi, those moments carried over into how she interacted with people. She learned early on, from her parents, a valuable lesson about treating others the way she wanted to be treated. The majority of people who came into contact with her saw just how pleasant she was. This life lesson overflowed into school, especially.

Many of the people that gravitated toward Naomi were ones who felt like they were an outcast. She never fully understood why this was the case because, to her, they were people who just wanted to be loved and shown compassion as she desired. Naomi enjoyed her private school upbringing for the most part because she saw it as an opportunity always to try to do her best. It was also at school that she learned what God's favor looked like in her life, and by following his lead, that nothing was ever impossible.

That all changed on one bright sunny Saturday morning at home. Naomi awakened to get ready for her day and remembered that Miguel, her classmate from Spanish class, was coming over. They were working on their group project.

Why must it be a group project?

I prefer to work alone because I know at least the work will get done.

Feelings of nervousness about Miguel coming over swirled around her head because of their previous interactions with each other. Their love-hate friendship consisted of Miguel always doing something to bother Naomi; everything from playfully throwing things to gently pushing her out of his way, and ideas along this nature. Many of her friends would say, "Miguel must like you for him to do those silly boy things." Naomi began to wonder if that was true but was confused by the other actions Miguel showed.

One day in class, before anyone arrived, Naomi sat at a desk practicing some words for homework as Miguel entered the room loudly, announcing himself.

Pulling up a chair next to her, he asked, "What are you working on?"

"Just going over the vocabulary words from the other night," Naomi replied.

"Well, let me help you," Miguel stated without really asking her if she wanted his help.

As they went over some words, Naomi began to feel Miguel's hand touching her knee. As he lightly stroked her knee, she could feel her body tense up. Naomi sat frozen, not quite sure what to say or even do. Suddenly the door slammed open, and Miguel's hand was back on his lap, and he was back up to his old tricks.

I am glad that it is over.

What the hell was that?

Naomi kind of liked Miguel, but this was new territory for her. She had heard the sex talk plenty of times, but nothing prepared her for what to do in this situation. For Miguel, this was not the last or final time, either. The day he played with Naomi's knee, and she did not stop him, sparked something in him to see how much further he could go.

Arriving another day to class early, Naomi decided to lay on the couch in the room for a moment. Closing her eyes, she did not notice Miguel come in and see her lying there. Walking over to her, he sat down near her head and placed it in his lap. Laying there against her better judgment, Naomi froze up again as Miguel began to rub on her back. At the same time, he continued to move his hand around, up under her sweatshirt, until he was caressing her. Naomi began to like the tingling feeling his touch was sending through her body.

Oh, God, please help-me.

I know this is wrong, but why does it feel so good.

Naomi was not sure who she could turn to for help and didn't believe she was courageous enough to speak up for herself. As the door opened, Miguel pushed Naomi off of him and began his reign of torture.

To Naomi's dismay, this behavior spilled over into outside of the classroom as well. Excited for their Spanish class to head out to a local restaurant for a field trip, Naomi ended up seated in the backseat of the car sandwiched between Miguel and another classmate of theirs. Shifting around, Naomi tensed up as she felt Miguel's hand start to wander up her shirt as he rubbed on the side of her body and began moving his hands down to squeeze her butt.

I am in the car with all these people.

I can't believe he is doing this here.

Miguel grabbed Naomi's jacket, which she had brought with her in case she got cold and placed it over her leg and his. Sliding his hand down to the front of her jeans, he slowly began to unzip Naomi's zipper. Once he got it down as far as he could go, Miguel used his fingers to explore her. As the only girl in the car, Naomi did not know who to turn to in this situation. Resisting Miguel as much as she could without making a huge scene, she believed that she just needed to take what was being dished out.

Keep your face from reacting to what he is doing.

Maybe he will stop soon. I hope no one notices what is going on.

Overwhelmed by the feelings of shame and embarrassment, the car ride to the restaurant could not end fast enough.

As they arrived, Naomi took a moment to fix her clothes as everyone piled out of the car. Making their way into the restaurant, she and her classmates walked up to the doors of the Spanish restaurant. Taking their seats around a large rectangular table, Naomi and her classmates each displayed their knowledge of what they learned in Spanish class as the waiter wrote their order. Finally distracted by something else Naomi was able to shift her focus on enjoying the food.

Once they all had finished their meal, they stood up and began to head back to the car. Seated in the same spots, Miguel grabbed Naomi's jacket again and started touching her again. As the car came to a stop, she could feel the eyes of everyone in the vehicle glancing over her. Although silent, Naomi could tell everyone felt the uncomfortable, awkward tension that was being released from within her.

He is getting out of control, and I feel so dirty.

What he is doing has got to stop!

These experiences filled Naomi with so much confusion. She was not sure why Miguel treated her sweet one moment and was so mean the next. When she found out that he was assigned to be her partner for their project, she was not sure what to expect.

Maybe he will not try anything in my home.

I mean, I must be safe here.

Naomi preferred just to work alone, but since those were her teacher's instructions, she knew that there was not much she could do about it. As she waited for him to arrive, the butterflies in her stomach began to flutter. She was starting to like the arousal feelings that his touch kept provoking from the depths of her, but she felt an unsettling sense of guilt as well.

Earlier that day, Naomi grabbed together all the supplies that she thought they would need and just waited for Miguel so they could get started. When he finally arrived at Naomi's house, he told his mom what time to pick him up and waved goodbye to let her know that he was okay. As Miguel entered the house, he politely introduced himself to Naomi's mom and even made small talk. Leaving them to work privately downstairs, Naomi's mom, Linda, headed up the stairs.

Since Miguel seemed a little quieter than usual, Naomi jumped in with leading their project because she did not want to spend all of her Saturday working on it. As they went over their plan, Miguel interrupted and suggested that they should move to the couch to be more comfortable. After shifting everything over, Naomi continued to discuss their report, and while in mid-sentence, he leaned in to kiss her. "I hope that was alright," Miguel said with that sly grin she had seen on his face before.

Oh, God! This can't be happening again.

Placing his hand on her leg, Miguel leaned in and gently kiss her neck. Naomi sat frozen, not knowing what to do.

If I call out for my mom, what would she think or say about me?

If I do nothing, maybe he would stop.

Her silence was the reason Miguel did not stop and was all the permission he needed to continue. He then proceeded to unbutton her jeans and slide his hand down through her layers of clothing. With his other hand, he moved her legs open, making room to slip his finger into her. Naomi sat quietly in disbelief while trying to figure out what to do while Miguel continued to have his way with her. He proceeded to put his body on top of her but stopped as the footsteps of her mother grew louder, coming downstairs. They both quickly fixed their clothes as Miguel whispered for Naomi not to tell anyone.

Her mother asked them if they were done at the same time Miguel's mother returned to pick him up. He politely said thank you for having him at their home. He left behind him some massive devastation in the form of an unfinished Spanish project and a heartbroken Naomi.

Racing up the stairs to her room, Naomi slammed the door shut behind her and fell facedown into her pillow. The tears began to flow like a stream from her eyes. The confusion between what her body was feeling, and her mind was saying made Naomi feel very unclean. She liked Miguel and thought that his actions were just how things were supposed to be displayed.

Why do I love it when he touches me?

My body gets hot, and my breathing gets short.

I know from what I have been taught, this is not right, though.

I should wait until marriage.

I don't understand how we got to this point or what I may have said to initiate this.

I am so confused.

Her mind raced, trying to find the answers to why this happened to her. Naomi thought back to the time they met to see if there was any indicator of something; she may have said, but for some reason, her memory was not allowing her access that day. Lately, it seemed like her mind was doing that more and more. Every time she would have a bad day, or if something traumatic happened to her, Naomi began to notice that her mind would completely erase the thought of it.

Growing up, her ability to recall it became so bad that her mother, Linda Johnson, and sister, Lily Johnson, would joke and say, "Don't ask Naomi because she won't remember." Those words burned so deep into Naomi's heart that she began to feel dumb and stupid. Wondering why her brain could not recall certain moments or memories, began to make her feel less smart than what she indeed was. Sitting up in her bed, Naomi hugged the pillow and began to sing softly to herself. Music was her saving grace whenever life seemed to be going wrong.

Clutching her pillow tightly, the thoughts of what happened began to make Naomi feel a strong desire to reach some sort of satisfaction. Images of how the situation could have played out if she and Miguel had not been interrupted began to dance around in her head as she turned onto her back and opened her legs. Overwhelmed with lustful thoughts and feelings, her hand started to make its way down her thigh and into her lips. Playing with herself had become a norm, especially when Naomi felt unloved or looked at sexually by someone. Once finished, an immediate feeling of shame and guilt washed over her causing Naomi to feel dirty inside.

I am so stupid for doing that.

Why did I have to touch myself?

It always seems like I can't help it even when I tell myself not to do it.

How else am I supposed to release the built-up tension?

From that day on, Naomi's trust, especially in boys and men, started to dwindle slowly. Little did she know that the same mistrust would begin to enter into her relationship with God too. Their sexual desire for her defined all her interactions with men from then on. Many of the men she met seemed only interested in two things: what Naomi looked like naked and how good she was in bed.

That is all you will ever be.

You are just an object of desire for them.

No one will ever love you and take you seriously.

A voice would continuously say to her. As Naomi internalized these thoughts, this became the way she saw herself, and she began to live out her life in this manner. If that is all men saw in her, then she needed to do something about it.

I will become what they see me.

Naomi is dead and no longer a part of who I am.

From now on, I will introduce myself as Mara Johnson.

Mara became Naomi's alter ego, who was secure in her sexuality. She was able to enjoy men and leave them just as quickly as they had done to her in the past. Opening herself up to the exploration of being willing to try anything once, Mara's mind began to desire and chase after the expression of love, which her heart genuinely began to crave. Choosing to walk away from the life she had always known, Mara started her journey into uncharted territory.

Ditch

Excited to head out to a house party which she had gotten invited to earlier that day, Mara searched through the items in her closet looking for an outfit that made her feel sexy but not too naked either. Grabbing her favorite blue top and skinny denim jeans, Mara also picked out her favorite pair of sneakers and earrings to complete the look. Heading into the shower, she began to wonder what the night would bring. Once dressed, she was ready to head out under cover of the dark of night. Finally arriving at the house party, Mara glanced around the room to see if she recognized anyone who was there.

Where is she?

She told me she would be here!

Hearing the notification ring go off on her phone, Mara saw the text message pop up that said, "Sorry, I can't make it. Something else came up."

Feeling her body temperature begin to get hot from her anger boiling within, Mara tried hard to forget that she just got stood up by her classmate who invited her. Heading over to the table that was set up with the liquor, Mara asked the young-looking man behind it for a drink.

"What would you like?" he asked.

"I'll have an Incredible Hulk," Mara replied as she gazed over the hard liquor which was sat out on the table.

"Coming right up," the young-looking man replied as he quickly mixed her up a drink. Handing it over to her, Mara began to take small sips until it gave her the liquid courage that she needed to interact with people. As the music began to play, Mara wanted to dance but not hold onto her drink all night. So, she gulped it down and began to dance. It was something she had enjoyed doing even when she was younger.

Swaying her hips from side to side, the rhythm of the music started to take over her body. Winding from left and right, the people in the room began to take notice, especially the attention of the owner of the apartment, Derrick, who stood by watching her from across the room. As Mara danced, more and more people began to make their way to the dance floor, but she could feel the eyes of Derrick following her body's every movement.

He is not bad looking.

Derrick's chocolate brown skin, dark brown eyes,

and tall height caused Mara to take notice. It was the confidence in his smile and the fact that he looked decently muscular from the T-shirt he was wearing, which made him even more intriguing to her. As the night progressed, Mara started to feel the weight of exhaustion setting in from dancing.

Making her way over to the door, which led to the outdoor patio, she found an empty chair and sat down. Closing her eyes and taking a deep breath, Mara took in the refreshing feeling of the fresh air and calmness of being away from all the action and people inside. "Hello Miss," said a deep alluring voice. Opening her eyes, she turned to look and saw this tall, muscular, chocolate man sitting in a chair next to her.

"Hello," she said back.

"My name is Derrick, and what is yours?" he said as he extended out his hand to shake hers.

"My name is Mara," she replied, wondering what he wanted because she had noticed him earlier that night staring at her.

"Well, first, let me ask, do you mind if I smoke?" he asked as he pulled out a wrapper and small bag of weed.

"No," she replied as Derrick rolled up two blunts quickly.

"Second, do you smoke, and would you like to join me?", asked Derrick locking his gaze directly into Mara's eyes.

"Yes, sure," answered Mara. Surprised by her

answer, Derrick reached into his pocket and pulled out a lighter.

Flicking back on the top of it to expose the flame, he placed the blunt to his mouth and lit it on fire. While pulling on it with his lips, he inhaled and made puff circles as he slowly exhaled. Then Derrick passed it to Mara, she placed the blunt to her lips, pulled in the smoke, and slowly opened her lips. As the smoke escaped, she began to inhale it through her nose again and finally blew it back out of her mouth. Mara could feel Derrick looking at her.

He is over there, probably thinking.

Dang, this is not the first time she has ever hit a blunt.

Derrick and Mara continued to do this for a while and talked about what seemed like everything. Their conversation flowed so nicely that they both forgot there were other people partying in the apartment. Looking at his watch, Derrick realized it was time to shut down the party before the neighbors started to complain. "Hey, Miss Lady, don't go anywhere. I need to end this party, but I would like to continue my conversation with you," said Derrick politely as he walked toward the door. As the door closed behind him, Mara could hear the music getting softer and the shuffling of feet. When Derrick returned, all she could hear was him saying goodbye to someone and to have them call him tomorrow.

"So, where were we?" asked Derrick, eager to find out more about Mara. Taking out the other blunt, he lit it up, started puffing on it, and passed it over to Mara.

I guess I can handle a little more.

Between that drink and these two blunts, I should be straight if I stop after this.

Continuing their conversation right where it had left off, time seemed to casually linger by as the two sat there enjoying the moment. Watching Mara fold her arms while rubbing them up and down, due to the brisk cold wind that blew past them, Derrick offered to head back into his apartment. Gently grabbing her hand, he led her onto the sofa where he sat down close next to her. Caressing her neck, Derrick looked deeply into the mesmerizing pools of her eyes and leaned into kiss Mara. With her defenses down, she allowed him to do all that he was thinking of doing to her from earlier that evening when he first spotted her on the dance floor.

Waking up to the rays of sunlight that pierced through the window, Mara began to rub her eyes and stretch. Scanning the room, she quickly noticed that it looked rather odd. She reached down to pull back the covers and was startled to find the naked man lying next to her. Putting together the pieces from the night before, Mara realized her clothes were spread across the floor.

Damn, I did it again.

What the hell is wrong with me.

I have got to stop drinking and smoking weed.

Interrupted by the loud snoring from the body lying next to her, Mara realized he was at least alive but sleeping very soundly.

What is his name?

I slept with him, and I can't even remember his name.

I have got to hurry up and get out of here before he wakes up.

Moving slowly out of bed to gather her clothes, Mara picked them up one by one and put them on quickly.

Where is my purse?

I know I had one with me.

Looking over the room one more time, Mara saw it nestled on the chair, which faced the bed. Gracefully walking on her tiptoes, like a ballet dancer, she picked up her purse, looked through it to make sure everything was there so she could run away from this situation as quickly as possible.

Running had become something Mara was good at along with one-night stands. It was easier for her to be the desire for someone's affection than create long-lasting relationships. After looking through her purse, Mara began to dig through the contents to locate her keys and phone.

"Hey, where are you headed?" called out the deep voice from the man in the bed, which startled her so bad that her heart felt like it skipped a beat.

"I have to get back home," she answered quickly, hoping he would sense the urgency in her voice.

"Mara, at least let me take you home, and before

we go, I have something for you," said the man as he leaped out of bed and walked into the bathroom.

Oh great!

What now and why can't I remember his name?

"Aww. Here it is," he said as he returned with a small square box in his hands and handed it over to Mara.

Reading the words on the box out loud, Mara saw it said *Morning After* as a confused look formed over her face. "Yeah, you know. We had a wild night, and you were damn good. It was fun and all, but I don't want a baby by you," he explained to her. Mara stared blankly due to the sting of these words but quickly remembered that she needed to get back home.

As he finished getting dressed, he grabbed his wallet and keys then extended his arm toward the door allowing Mara to lead. Mara could tell that he was getting one last good look at her butt while she walked away in front of him. Processing the emotions of what he had just said, a toxic mixture of shame, embarrassment, and anger began to form. It was not the time to let these feelings out.

"Do you have all of your things?" he asked while reaching out to open the door for her.

"Yes, I do," Mara replied as she walked out the door and into the hallway of the apartment complex.

Heading toward his car, Derrick opened the door for Mara to get in. As he pulled out of the parking space, he turned on the radio as they began the drive back to campus. Seated in an uncomfortable silence so thick that it could be cut with a knife, Mara stared out the window watching the houses, trees, and people pass by. Pulling up to the road, which led to her dorm, Derrick parked, walked around to the other side, and opened her door. Swinging her legs out of the car, Mara looked up at Derrick.

"Call me some time, and don't forget to take that pill," said Derrick as leaned down to hug her. Shutting the door behind her, he walked around to the driver's side of the car, hopped in, and drove off. Walking to her dorm, Mara began to feel so dirty.

Not only did she need to take a shower to remove his scent but, more importantly, the shame. Walking up the steps to her dorm and finally making it into her room, Mara grabbed a bottle of water from the mini fridge, opened the box of Morning After, and placed the pill on her tongue.

Bottoms up, I guess.

Swallowing the pill and chasing it with water, she made her way to the bathroom, undressed, and stepped into the shower. Letting the warm water roll down her neck, shoulders, and the rest of her body, Mara, began to reflect on what transpired the night before.

I'm so stupid.

Why didn't I just say no?

Why didn't I just leave when everyone else did?

I am so mad.

Struggling to recall everything that happened,

flashes of certain moments began to play in her head. Feeling Derrick inside of her and gripping her hips tightly as he pulled them closer to him, caused Mara to close her eyes and relive that moment. As she let out a moan while in the shower, Mara realized that she needed to get over what took place the other night. She knew Derrick didn't love her and that he did not want to continue seeing her. Derrick had already gotten what he wanted from her. Now it was over.

Stepping out of the shower, Mara wrapped her towel around herself and walked back into her room. Looking for some pajamas, she began to feel the all too familiar spirit looming over her. This dark cloud of heaviness started to form within her mind. Trying to shake it off, Mara continued to get dressed and grabbed the remote to turn on the television. Flipping through the channels to find something distracting on, she finally decided on one of the home designs shows she enjoyed watching.

Seeing a flash on her phone, Mara saw two text messages come into her phone. Clicking on the envelope button to open them, she saw they both were from her friend, Jason. The first message said, "Hey, what are you doing?" and the second said, "Worried about you, call me back." Right now, was not the time to call Jason back because Mara did not want to be bothered. She was content wallowing in her salty emotions from the wrong decision that she made.

I will call Jason tomorrow.

Putting her phone on do not disturb, she laid down in her bed and continued to watch the show. Mara was not in the mood to be bothered and just wanted to take this time and not think about anything. As she lay in bed, Mara saw her phone begin to ring. Glancing down at it, she saw the name came up as Jason.

Should I pick it up or let it go to voicemail?

On the third ring, Mara was convinced just to pick up and see what he wanted.

"Hey, Jason?" answered Mara.

"Hey, what is up with you? Where have you been? Did you get my texts?" replied Jason, a little frustrated that Mara did not respond to any of his text messages.

"Not much. I am just in my dorm watching television. What are you up to?" answered Mara, trying to avoid explaining why she did not want to respond to his texts.

Not wanting to run her off, Jason decided to let go of his interrogative questioning and just allow Mara to talk to him. He cared for her as a friend but wondered what it would be like to be more than that. He also had heard about some guys she had slept with and given his advice about it. When she was like this, he enjoyed being the one to hold her but, wondered if there could be more. Mara had always liked Jason's company and enjoyed spending time with him. She never desired for her corrupt and sinful ways to change or mess up their friendship or the type of person he was. She always tried to keep a little distance between them so he would not become just another number in her life.

"So, how are you doing?" asked Jason, concerned for Mara.

"Not so good. This man had sex with me and gave me a "morning after" pill. I have never felt so bad in my life. Like what in the hell was I thinking," replied Mara as the words poured out from her lips.

"Mara, how many times have I told you that you are beautiful, and you don't have to live like this. You could probably have any man you wanted. Just pick that one and let him wait on getting sex cause once we get some, we did not want to date you, then we are gone," replied Jason trying to help educate her by shining a light on how men would view the situation. As silence fell upon their conversation, Jason gave Mara a minute to think about what he said.

He knew just how she liked to process through things and wanted to give her the space to do so.

"Mara are you still there?" asked Jason after feeling like he had waited enough.

"Yes. Just thinking about what you said," answered Mara with a sadness in her voice.

"Do you need some company tonight? I mean, at least you will not be alone with your thoughts," asked Jason, hoping to just get a chance to hold her or be near to her.

"Sure, why not? How quickly can you come through?" asked Mara because if it would take him more than an hour, she was just going to shut the invitation down.

"I am in my dorm and can be to you in the next 10 to 15 minutes. How does that sound?" asked Jason while getting ready on the phone to try to cut the time he quoted down to half. Throwing quickly on a pair of dark denim jeans, a crimson red t-shirt, some tennis shoes, and spraying a little cologne on his neck, he headed out the door of his dorm.

"Sounds fine. I will see you then and call me when you get here," replied Mara as she hung up the call.

Getting up out of bed, she took off her pajamas and looked for a shirt and a pair of shorts to put on instead. Sitting back on her bed, Mara went back to watching the new television program that came on. It did not take long for her phone to ring and Jason to say he was outside. Taking her time getting down the stairs, Mara opened the door to let him in. Walking up the stairs behind her, Jason could not help but enjoy the view that her shorts were providing him. The shorts Mara wore allowed him to have a sneak peek of the bottom of her butt cheek without being too revealing.

Trying desperately to control himself, he hated that there were plenty of times that he had to remind himself that he was just her friend and nothing more. Hearing about how she was continually giving herself away so freely to other men, he had wondered why she had not done the same to him. It was more recently that Jason had thought how nice it would be for Mara to just jump on top of him and whisper in his ear that she wanted him right now. He already knew that if the moment ever presented itself, the chances of him stopping it might be slim to none, but right now was just content to be in her presence.

Making their way up the stairs to her room, Mara opened the door and sat down on her bed. About to ask where he should sit, Mara interjected his thought and said: "Come sit next to me." Responding quickly, he took a seat next to her on the bed.

"So, talk to me and tell me what happened with this guy?" asked Jason trying to get Mara to open up more about what happened.

"Well, you know I got invited to this house party. I went and ended up drinking then smoked some weed. I should have known then that I needed to go and head back home. The guy who owned the place was staring at me while I was dancing, he started to talk with me, and I smoked with him. It seemed like everything was fine until he cleared out the place. Next thing I know, we were on the couch, the bed, the floor, the shower, and in a chair," said Mara, ready to express and let go of what had happened.

The image of Mara doing whatever she did to that guy began to flash in his mind, and the fact that she was looking good in those shorts with her thighs visible to him was not helping him to focus on their friendship at that moment. Holding himself together, Jason tried to think about other things.

"See, Mara, this is what I have told you before and keep telling you. You don't have to do all that. You are mysteriously sexy, and some guys would be honored to get to know you first," said Jason as he expressed his own feelings while hiding them behind, trying to provide advice to her. Looking up into his eyes, Mara gave him a look that made him even weaker in the knees.

"Oh, really now. So, why do I keep falling for these types of guys?" asked Mara, wondering if his male perspective would shine some light on her destructive behavior. Feeling his insides begin to get hot, Jason tried to calm down his flesh carefully, but it was starting to get harder and harder to handle. Knowing that he should probably leave, Jason continued to sit and try to talk with Mara.

"Mara, I don't know. To be quite honest with you, I wish you would not do this anymore," replied Jason as he warred within himself to just stay in the friend zone or answer the call that his body was feeling.

Something is different about Jason today, but I can't put my finger on what it is. He usually is not this weird around me. Shaking off the thought, Mara listened to his answer and continued to carry on the conversation.

"Why do you say you wish I would not do this anymore?" asked Mara, curious to find out his reasoning behind what he said.

"You deserve better," he answered as he moved closer to her.

Unable to contain himself any further, he swiftly pulled her close to his body and began to kiss her passionately. Surprised by how nice the kiss was and the utter shock of what was happening, Mara began to forget it was Jason and melted a little into his arms. Unzipping his jeans, he revealed himself to her, and just as quickly with his other hand. Jason began to remove her shorts and panties as he prepared to slide his finger into her.

No, this is wrong.

I have got to fight back this time.

We are friends, or at least I thought we were.

Pushing back on his arm as he wrapped himself around her, Mara yelled, "No, Stop! We can't do this."

Breathing heavy, Jason answered, "Can't do what Mara. You have given it to other men who didn't know you as I know you. Just let me get a taste."

Using her arms and legs to push him off of her, Mara fought back, not knowing if things were going to get worse or not. Having more strength than her, he had the advantage to take what he wanted from her. All Jason had to do was put his weight on her body, and this fight would have been over. Hoping that he would find it within himself to do the right thing and not force her to give him her body, Mara did the only thing she could think of, which was to pray.

Father God, if you can hear me.

Please help me.

Mara had not prayed or spoken to God in a long

time. Especially not since that day that she chose to walk away from him, but today God was the only person she could think to call on. Even if she called out for help from someone else, Mara knew they saw her invite Jason in and would probably not also take her seriously just because of what they assumed the situation was.

Immediately after her prayer, Jason returned to his senses. Looking down into her eyes, he could see the fear and new mistrust Mara now had for him. Unwrapping himself from around her, Jason stood up and began to fix his clothes. Sitting up, Mara pulled her legs up to her chest while intently watching Jason's every move. Not quite knowing what had changed within him, she felt the need to brace herself in the event he thought about trying anything else. Picking up her panties and shorts, he handed them to Mara without even looking at her.

"Damn," said Jason, realizing the access he had as her friend was now being revoked and all that was going to be lost because of what he tried to do.

Finding the courage to speak, Mara pointed to the door and said, "Jason, you have to leave. Also, please lose my number."

Standing up to put back on her clothes, Jason glanced at her butt one last time and headed for the door. Walking down the stairs out of her dorm, he headed to the front main entrance door and continued his journey back to his dorm. In shock, Mara could not believe what had happened. Not only were her actions chipping away at her self-esteem, but she was now losing friends in the process.

I can't keep living like this.

I don't know what I have to do, but there has got to be something better.

Reflecting on these two incidents, Mara entered a mental space that she did not want to be in. Looking for the number on her phone of the guy who sold liquor on campus to everyone who could not go and get it, Mara found it and dialed. She never knew his name, only that to protect himself from what he was doing, he asked everyone to refer to him as "the drink man." Mara had ordered from him plenty of times before to the point where she had become one of his regular customers. He had a pretty good memory and could recall what her favorite drinks were.

"Hey, Ma. What's good? What would you like to order?" said the male voice on the phone.

"Not much. Can I get a small bottle of whatever hard liquor you have on you right now?" said Mara, ready to drown all her troubles and problems into a glass of something.

"Sure. I got you, and I remember what you have ordered. So, I'll bring you something," the guy on the other line said.

"Cool, how much do I owe you?" answered Mara, who knew he never was handing out drinks for free because it cost him something even to get it.

"For you, nothing. As long as you come out and have a quick drink with me and maybe a puff on a blunt if you are up for it," replied the voice on the phone. Pausing on the telephone, Mara realized that nothing was free, and all things had a motive attached to it, but it was getting beyond ridiculous.

I just want this drink, and some weed because I am thinking about saying yes.

Talking to herself, Mara began to weigh the pros and cons. After the day she had, she figured what more do I have to lose.

"Sure. When will you be here?" answered Mara. "Soon. I will give you a call when I arrive," answered the male voice.

"Alright," replied Mara as she hung up the phone.

Changing out her shorts for jeans, she gathered her keys and wallet. Locating one of her purses, she placed everything in it and waited by the phone. Suddenly the phone rang with the name the drink man across the screen. Picking up the call, Mara answered.

"Meet me outside," said the male voice.

"Alright. I am heading out now," replied Mara.

Locking up her room, Mara made her way down the stairs and stepped outside to see him sitting in his car. Walking over, he opened the window while signaling for her to get in.

Dark Clouds of Depression

Stumbling slowly back up the stairs of her dorm, Mara opened up the door to her room, walked over to her bed and plopped down on top of it. Too tired to change her clothes, she grabbed her blanket and just laid there. As Mara laid there, her mind began to drift off into a dream. Watching herself rocking back and forth in her closet as she hugged her knees. The build-up of tears burst forth from her eyes like a dam which had broken due to the pressure. Closing her eyes, she could see the image again, which had haunted her many times before the rope tied up as a noose with her body dangling from it.

NOT AGAIN.

NO, NO, NO!

The battle in her mind sometimes waged constant war within her, which at times was so intense that Mara even thought about writing out her suicide note. Being seen as nothing more than a sex toy had seeped so deep into her soul that she believed that was all she was.

Who could love a person like me?

It makes more sense for me just to become a prostitute than enter into a loving relationship.

The past year of sexual experiences had begun to weigh heavily on Mara's heart but especially her mind. She was becoming numb to love as if it was a made-up emotion or action, and her trust for men, people, and even God started fading away like the passing of time that can't be returned. Little did Mara know, but her identity was in the process of being reformed, not for good but evil.

Her view of the world around her started to look so blurry that she had no clue of what was truly real or apparent. Rocking back and forth in her closet, Mara saw herself in such a vulnerable state but was loudly interrupted by the ringing sound coming from her phone lying on her bed next to her. Waking up from her sleep and able to regain a sense of where she was, Mara recognize the assigned ringtone as the one for her mother, and she debated within herself on answering the call.

What will she think of me?

I don't want to talk with her.

Not now. Not yet.

She will just judge me if I tell her and ask me why I did what I have did?

I don't even have a good reason to give her.

Hearing her stomach growl, Mara began to feel hungry and realizing she needed to get out of the bed to get something to eat. Deciding not to share the troubling thoughts with her mother, Mara picked up her phone and saw one missed call and seven text messages from Linda. Quickly scanning through the text messages, she saw one who said, "Call me back, and I know you need someone to talk to."

Her mother, Linda, had always been able to sense when her daughter needed her or when things were not right. Mara was the same way but never really understood why they both were sensitive like that at times. As the suicidal feelings began to subside, Mara debated what to do first.

Order food to be delivered to my dorm or call back my mom. Decisions. Decisions.

Hearing her stomach growl louder, she realized it might be better to order the food first, and while waiting for it to show, call her mother back. Searching through the internet on her phone, she quickly dials the pizza place not far from campus.

"Hello, thank you for calling the House of Pizza. May I take your order?" said the cracking male voice on the other line.

"Yes, please. I would like a personal combo pizza without the sausage," replied Mara.

"Personal combo with no sausage got it! Will that complete your order?" answered the voice on the other line.

"Yes, that is all!" said Mara. "Your total is $13.50, and we will have that delivered in about 45 minutes," said the voice.

"Alright, see you then," replied Mara as she hung up the phone.

Time to call my mom and have this conversation.

Searching for her mother's missed call, Mara took a deep breath as she pressed the telephone icon button. Waiting for the ringing to stop made something in Mara wants to hang up. Just as she was about to press the hang-up button, she heard a voice on the other line say

"Hello. Hi, Mom. It's me, Naomi," said Mara in a timid voice. She could not call herself Mara to the woman who gave birth to her and took time out to choose her name.

"Naomi, why did you not answer my phone call earlier?" asked Linda jumping right into the conversation, trying to find out just what her daughter was up doing.

"Well, Mom, if you must know, I was kind of having a rough moment earlier," said Mara with a tone of sadness in her voice.

"I could sense that, so I called you. Are you alright?" questioned Linda hoping a softer approach would allow her daughter Naomi to share what was going on.

When Naomi first left for college, Linda would hear from her at least three to four times a week, but lately, those calls had dwindled to twice or less per week. Linda already knew that when life became too much for Naomi or when there was something wrong, her daughter would always retreat to a safe space of isolation.

"Mom, I am fine. There are just some things going on in my head that I have to deal with and sort out," replied Naomi in her usual roundabout way when she wanted to avoid sharing what she was thinking.

"Well... Alright, Naomi. Know that I love you, your father loves you, your sister loves you, and more importantly, God loves you too," replied Linda, unsure of what else to say and not wanting to risk her daughter trying to rush her off of the phone.

Hearing a beeping sound in her phone, Mara pulled the phone away from her ear and looked at the name of the incoming call. It flashed "House of Pizza."

"Hey Mom, hold on really quick," requested Mara.

Clicking over to catch the other phone call, Mara answered, "Hello."

"Hey Mara, your order is here. I am downstairs at the front door of your dorm," said the male voice.

"Alright, I am heading down now," replied Mara. Grabbing the money from her wallet and her key, Mara headed out the door.

Dang, my mom is on the other line.

Locating the button to switch back to her call, Mara, as she inhaled and exhaled deeply, "Hey, Mom. Sorry about that. I ordered a pizza, and the delivery guy just arrived. I will talk with you later," said Mara, slightly out of breath as she raced down the stairs toward the front door of the dorm.

"Alright, Naomi. I will talk with you later. You have a good night," replied Linda realizing this was not the time to give her daughter a lecture on anything but just to allow her to open up when she was ready.

"You too, Mom," answered Mara as she hung up the phone.

Finally, arriving at the main door of the dorm, Mara opened the door and let in the delivery guy.

"Here is your combo pizza with no sausage. That will be $13.50," he said.

Handing him a $20 while he gave her the pizza, he started to count out her change.

"Just keep the change for your tip," Mara said as she began to realize just how hungry she was and that she was ready to be alone.

"Thanks," said the delivery guy as he smiled and turned to leave.

"No problem," replied Mara as she made sure the door was closed behind him then turned to head back upstairs to her room and eat.

Finally, back in her room, Mara sat down on the bed and opened up the lid of the pizza box. Grabbing a slice of pizza, she placed it into her mouth. Looking for the remote which had found itself wrapped up in the sheets of her bed, Mara turned on the television so the sound of other people talking could bring a sense of comfort.

Why did you do that?

You knew that man only wanted sex from you.

Why could you not say no?

Not able to escape the thoughts that began racing around in her head, Mara began to feel the weight of shame from sleeping with men who truly cared nothing for her. Realizing the only thing all the men had in common was, they saw her as an easy target for one night of pleasure, and Mara could feel the embarrassment starting to transform itself into a rage.

How in the hell did I allow this to get this far?

All of those men, some I remember their names and others I don't.

All I can recall is that when I would drink and smoke that I became someone new. Almost like an alter ego.

Reflecting on everything that had taken place, Mara could tell something about her was always different when she had sex. Typically, a shy introverted person, she would morph in this unapologetic, insatiable sex goddess who was good at what she did. Therefore, many of those men remembered her name and the night they were together better than Mara could. Not ready to face what she had done, Mara picked up her phone and began to scroll through it.

Seeing a photo of an ad with the image of an airplane, Mara began to think about her family. She missed them and wondered if any school holidays were coming up soon. Locating the calendar on her phone, she opened it up and saw that there was a two-week-long one coming up. Switching back between the tabs, Mara clicked on the ad to check out the prices for flights. The flights from Georgia to California that she found for those two weeks would cost around $350 for a round trip ticket.

Tomorrow I need to call my mom and talk with her about the price and see how quickly I can book the flight.

Maybe a different environment will do me good.

Perhaps I just need to get away from here for a little while so I can come back better.

Looking at the pizza box, Mara saw that she had some slices left. Wrapping them up to save them for later, she placed them into the fridge for another day. Heading into the bathroom, she brushed her teeth and washed her face.

It has been a long day. I am ready to call it a night.

Walking back out of the bathroom, Mara let out a yawn. Opening the dresser drawer, she grabbed a fresh set of pajamas. She crawled into bed as she dozed off with the television still talking in the background.

Nervous and excited to speak with her mother about the flight home she found, Mara woke up refreshed to see another day. She was hopeful that her mother, Linda, would not find the price too expensive for a two-week stay. Realizing that she would need to wait a few hours before calling her mother due to the time difference, Mara looked around to see what else needed to be done. Cleaning her room as she waited patiently for time to past, Mara finally dialed her mother's number.

"Hello, Naomi," answered her mother, wondering what the reason for this phone call was but grateful at the same time that her daughter did not distance herself from her.

"Hey, Mom. How are you doing today?" replied Mara searching for the words to ask about what she wanted.

"I am well, and how are you doing today?" asked Linda, not quite sure where this conversation was going.

"I am better. So, mom, I wanted to ask you about something," said Mara as she mustered up the courage to just come out and say what she wanted.

"Of course, go ahead," replied Linda bracing herself for whatever was going to come out of Mara's mouth.

Feeling a little courage rise within her, Mara finally blurted out that she wanted to go home for a visit. Sharing with her mother the details of what she researched, Mara shared with Linda the round-trip flight for $350 and the fact that school was going to out for two weeks soon. Grateful coming home was all her daughter was calling to tell her, Linda quietly thanked God and thought about it for a moment.

"That sounds doable. I knew a school holiday was coming up, and we wanted to get you to come home for it. So, I am glad you asked. I will let your father know, and I want you to book the flight. I will just move some money over to your account so that you can pay for it," said Linda, excited to be able to see her daughter. Promising herself that she would hug Naomi extra tight when she got a chance to see her because she knew something was going on even though Naomi had not shared a whole lot.

"Well, mom. Thank you. I miss home and you guys," said Mara relieved that the conversation went over well.

She was also excited to be able to have a change in her environment in a few weeks because she was not getting it right at all. It seemed like every opportunity that was presented to Mara of smoking weed, drinking, or sex; she was accepting it like medicine or candy. Knowing none of those things were good for her, it seemed like every time she tried to do better in her strength, Mara quickly would lose the battle.

Maybe the trip home will give me a change of perspective.

Maybe all I need to do is just get away from all the temptations.

Seeing the flash of light on her phone, Mara looked down and saw a text message on her phone. Scanning it, she saw that it was from her mother, Linda. As she opened it, Mara saw written, "Check your account. The money is there for you to book your flight," Grabbing her laptop from her desk, Mara logged in and opened the webpage of her bank. Typing in her username and password, she immediately saw the transfer of funds that her mother had moved into her account.

Excited to know that she would be able to head home in a soon, Mara opened another tab and proceeded to book her flight. After receiving her confirmation code and the time of the flight's arrival, Mara texted her mother back with all the details. "Sounds great. Can't wait to see you," texted back her mother. Breathing out a heavy sigh, Mara began to believe that maybe there was still hope for her and life itself.

After obtaining her boarding pass and moving through the security checkpoints, the day had finally arrived for Mara to head back home. Filled with excitement to finally get away from the chaotic, drama-filled life she had created for herself, Mara was eager to try again and start over. Boarding the plane, she settled into her seat and placed the headphones over her ears to listen to some music.

Grabbing a piece of gum out of her carryon bag, Mara put it into her mouth and began to chew, which had become her ritual every time right before the plane began to take off. She never cared for how the change in altitude made her ears feel clogged, so to deal with the situation, she would always chew a piece of gum until the plane would stabilize, and her hearing restored to normal.

Finally, in the air, Mara began to doze off, taking brief short naps as she traveled across the country to make it home. Waking up from one of her naps, Mara was filled with anticipation as the captain informed them that they were preparing to land. Ready to get up and stretch her legs, the plane made its descent down onto the runway. As the plane came to a complete stop, Mara was more than ready to exit it. Grabbing her carryon bag and checking the space around her, she moved into the aisle and walked in the line of people leaving the plane.

Then Mara headed to pick up the rest of her luggage. Following those that seemed to know where they were going, Mara double-checked her flight number to help identify which carousel her luggage was going to be. Seeing her bag emerge, Mara grabbed it and walked over to a bench to sit down. Locating her phone, she turned off the airplane mode and dialed her mom, Linda's number. Hearing it ring, Mara waited for her mother to pick up but heard an all too familiar voice shout out to her.

"Naomi! Naomi!" shouted Lily, who was wildly waving her arms to get Mara's attention. Not far behind Lily trailed both of their parents, Linda and Edward Johnson. Opening up her arms, Linda hugged Naomi.

"I am glad that you are home," said Linda.

"I am glad too," replied Mara.

"Is this everything?" Edward asked, ready to get everyone to the car.

"Yes, it is," answered Mara.

Helping her carry her bags, they walked and talked

on their way to where the car was parked. Finally, approaching their vehicle, Edward lifted up the trunk. He placed the bag into it while Linda, Lily, and Naomi got into the car. As Edward opened the door of the driver's side and got in, he set out for home. The drive home helped Mara to reflect on her life in college.

Maybe while I am back home, I can be Naomi again.

Well, at least to my parents and sister.

Pulling up into the driveway, they all exited the car and helped bring Mara's bags into the house. Heading up the stairs to her childhood room, Mara placed her bags down and laid on the bed. The slight feeling of jet lag was beginning to set in, which caused her to feel tired.

I will take a short nap.

Then I will have some energy in case my family wants to go out tonight.

Sitting back up long enough to locate her phone and charger, Mara plugged them in and rolled over to lay back down.

Waking up right before time for dinner, Mara grabbed a towel and headed into the bathroom to get a shower. Emerging dressed and ready, she passed Lily in the hallway, who was headed to her room.

"Hey, Lily. What is everyone doing for dinner?" asked Mara, trying to gather what her family was up to after being asleep for a few hours.

"Well, mom and dad mentioned going out to eat, so I would just check with them to see if that is what they want to do?" replied Lily as she continued into her room.

Heading down the stairs to the living room, Mara saw her mom, Linda sitting in the kitchen.

"Hey mom, I just passed Lily in the hallway, and I asked her if you all had plans for dinner. She told me to ask you or dad," shared Mara with her mother to figure out what her evening was going to include.

"Your father and I would like to take Lily and you out to eat. Is there any particular place you would like to go?" asked Linda, trying to figure out where they were going to go.

"I am not quite sure what I want so anything would be fine with me," replied Mara.

"Alright, then. I am just waiting on your father and sister to finish getting ready. We can head out to eat," informed Linda as she picked up her phone to research which restaurant she would like to go to.

Finally making their way down the stairs, Edward and Lily appeared around the corner and sat down on the sofa.

"Are we all ready to go?" asked Edward as he pulled out his keys from his pocket.

"Yes, we are. Naomi and I were just waiting for you and Lily. While we were waiting, I found a restaurant and even made a reservation. If we leave now, we can make it by then," said Linda as she was looking down at the time on her phone.

Gathering their things, the Johnson family all

headed out the garage door and into the car on their way to enjoy some good food and each other's company. As the Johnson family got back in the car to head home, Mara kept playing on her phone with her mind in her world. Feeling a little distant from everyone, thoughts of her lifestyle replayed in Mara's head. She began to feel bad because she was not taught to behave this way. Raised where attending church was the norm and having access to an excellent private school education should have set the standard for what her life was supposed to be modeled after when she went away for college.

Trying to figure out where her life took a wrong turn seemed to consume her mind that she did not even notice the car stop back in the garage of the Johnson family home. Observing her daughter, Linda could tell that something was not right with her, but she honestly could not put her finger on exactly what was wrong. As everyone walked back into the house, Linda walked side by side with Mara and asked if she could come out to the backyard and talk with her in about an hour.

Oh no, what did I do?

I can't believe I am terrified of having a conversation with my mother.

I just wish I knew what she would like to talk about.

Heading upstairs, Mara went into her room and saw her phone light up with a notification. Looking at her phone, she saw a message from Thomas. Since meeting online, Mara enjoyed that they just continued to talk over email and how Thomas expressed himself through written words. She was not falling in love but found herself intrigued by him. While responding to his email, Mara remembered her meeting with her mother.

Typing up her final thought and pressing send, she headed back down the stairs toward the backyard. Seated on the outdoor sofa was her mother, Linda, who was looking through her phone while she waited for Mara to arrive.

"Hey mom, you wanted to talk to me," said Mara stating the obvious because she was not quite sure about what her mother wanted to speak with her.

The thought had quickly crossed her mind that her mother would probably want to bring up the night they talked on the phone when she dreamt about committing suicide. Sitting down on the sofa opposite her mother, Mara took a deep breath to brace herself for whatever was to come.

"Mara, to be quite honest, I am not sure how to even address what I want to speak with you about. All I know is that you have changed, and I can tell. The young lady your father and I dropped off at college is not the same person I see seated across from me. Now, don't get me wrong, I knew that college would change you because it changes everyone for better or worse, but…" said Linda trailing off, not knowing how to say what she wanted to express carefully.

"Naomi, you don't seem like yourself at all. It is

almost as if the light that was in your eyes before you left has started to dim. Please let me know if I am on the right track?" asked Linda hoping her daughter would jump into this, and a discussion or at least two-way conversation would be formed.

"Well, you are right that my outlook on life has changed, and I have become a different person. I just went to college with a certain set of expectations that were shattered instantaneously, and this caused me frustration. So, I did feel the loss and was not sure how or even where I fit in. Finding my footing became overwhelming. Also, add the homesickness I was feeling. So, yeah. You were not far off at all," answered Mara carefully, not sure if she could share the raw truth of her emotions right now. Not that she did not trust her mother but wanted to avoid being judged or misunderstood desperately.

Changing the subject, Linda knew that for Naomi to speak that much about a topic meant that she said what she was going to reveal for now. "So, I saw you on your phone, giggling to yourself while we were at dinner. Do you mind sharing what that was about?" asked Linda jokingly but also curious to find out. "Well, there is this guy, but it is too early to know what this even is," answered Mara.

"Alright, just continue to keep yourself safe, and I mean physically, mentally, and spiritually. Well, it is getting late, and I am going to turn in," said Linda as she stood up and walked back into the house.

Sitting there a moment, Mara reflected over what just happened.

That was not as bad as I thought it was going to be.

It really could have been much worse.

Looking down at her phone, Mara saw another notification from Thomas. Smiling to herself, she opened it up and read the message. It said, "Hey, babe! I was just thinking of you. I can't wait for the day when I can be more to you than this. I dream of one day making you my wife. Love, Thomas." Heading back into the house and up the stairs, Mara changed her clothes and laid in bed, thinking about how to respond to Thomas's message.

Deep in Despair

A combination of nervousness and excitement crept into Mara's stomach as she opened her eyes and realized that the big day was finally here. It seemed like time was standing still during the months of planning, but as this day approached, it felt like time was moving at an acceleration that she was not quite prepared for. This was the day that she would become Mrs. Naomi Mara Porter.

Wow, two years passed by so quickly from meeting online to dating to Thomas asking me to marry him and now today.

I know I should probably be over the moon happy and excited, but I can't quite shake this strange feeling of am I doing the right thing.

She and Thomas had experienced a lot of ups and downs just to make it this point. Maybe this was where that strange sinking feeling was coming from. Stretching her arms high above her head, Mara began to push herself toward the head of the bed so she could rest her back on it.

Thomas and I are ready for this day.

I am excited to become his wife.

Mara began to think about everything they had planned and done for their wedding. Trying to locate her phone, Mara felt around in the covers and eventually grabbed it. Checking for the time, she saw that it read 7:30 AM.

Perfect.

I have time to get something to eat.

Go over my last-minute checklist and get to the church on time.

Laughing to herself at that last thought, Mara swung her legs out of bed, stood up and made her way to the kitchen. Opening the door to the fridge, Mara scanned it for some eggs, turkey bacon, grits, and orange juice. Knowing that their wedding would be taking place at a time between lunch and dinner, Mara knew that she would eventually be hungry later that day. So, a big southern-style breakfast it was. Opening the cabinets, Mara bent down and grabbed two frying pans and some pots. Cooking up everything that she pulled from out of the fridge, Mara made enough food for her father, mother, and sister.

"Come on, Johnson's family. Breakfast is ready!" Mara called out from the kitchen. Slowly emerged, her father, Edward, who enjoyed the food and was always ready to eat.

"So, today is the day. Are you ready?" he said as he sat down in one of the chairs at the circular table in the kitchen.

"I am nervous. Is that normal?" Naomi asked as she continued to set the table.

"Yes, that is normal," answered Edward even though he had been worried about his daughter getting married.

He wondered if she would be able to handle the responsibility as well as Thomas and if they would work well together as they figure their way through it. Finally, making their way into the kitchen came Lily, followed by Linda. Pulling out their chairs, both sat down and looked at the food which Mara had cooked.

"This looks good, Mara," said Lily, excited to start eating.

"Yes, I agree this does look good. Let us say grace," interjected Linda as Lily reached over to begin placing food on her plate.

"Edward, would you please lead us in a word of prayer," directed Linda.

"Um... Let Naomi do it because today is her big day," replied Edward.

"Alright, then. Naomi, please lead us in prayer," Linda said with a sense of frustration in her voice.

"Sure. Dear Heavenly Father, thank you for this food we have received. Please bless the hands that prepared and cultivated it. Be with me today as I get married before you. Please allow my union to bless not only for me but Thomas as well. Grant all who are coming to the wedding, traveling grace and mercy. In Jesus' name, I pray. Amen," said Mara as she prayed the words which flowed out from within her.

"Let's eat!" said Lily, who was more than eager to jump in and start eating.

"So, sis. Are you ready for today?" asked Lily in between chewing bites of her food.

"You know what? I am a little nervous, but I hope that is only normal for every or at least most brides to feel this way," answered Mara.

"Well, there are some last-minute things that need to get done. I just got a call from the printers that said the programs are ready to be picked up," said Linda.

"So, who can go and pick that up? I must stay here and at least get to the church on time. Is there anyone we can call?" inquired Mara trying somehow to find a solution.

"I think your godparents were planning on stopping by early to spend some time with us before the wedding. Maybe, I can ask them if they would be able to help us out," said Linda as she excused herself from the table and dialed Mara's godparent's number to call and find out.

Walking back into the kitchen, Linda had a calm look on her face. Mara wondering what was said, as she sat in anticipation for what was the answer.

"They can do it and are on the way right now. Once they get here, they will head to the printers to pick up the programs!" said Linda as she beamed with pride that this situation was handled.

Thank goodness.

I was hoping that I did not have to worry about this at all today.

Mara did not want anything else to go wrong because she was already feeling nervous and excited. This was the biggest decision she ever made and could not help but wonder if she was making the right one. As each one of them finished up the last piece of food on their plate, the doorbell chimed, and Mara ran over softly to the peephole to see who it was.

Sure enough, it was her godparents here to not only attend her wedding but save the day by picking up the programs. Heading off in Linda's car, Mara's godfather set out for the drive to the printers. Sitting on the sofa, Mara's godmother and mother, Linda, began to talk with one another and have one of their catch up with each other's life conversations. Moving the dishes into the sink, Mara and Lily quickly worked together to clean up the kitchen.

"I can't believe you're getting married before me," said Lily teasing Mara.

"I know, right. To be honest, I really thought that you would be the first one to get married out of both of us. Quite frankly, I thought I would be wandering around trying to figure my life out," replied Mara trying not to overthink her life.

"Well, we need to head out to the church in about

an hour," reminded Lily.

"Yes, so let me double-check that I have everything, and let's ride over there together," replied Mara.

Returning to her room, Mara placed her wedding dress on the bed, grabbed the box, which had her shoes and the bag which contained her jewelry and veil. Gathering all her things, Mara headed out to the car and draped her them gently onto the backseat. Lily raced out of the garage door with her dress and hung it up in the back of the car then placed her bag on the floor of the passenger side.

The two of them hopped into the car and rode out to the church. Pulling up to the church parking lot, Lily and Mara stepped out of the car, placed their things over their arms then headed toward the changing room for her and her bridesmaids.

While sitting in her chair, Mara tried to sit very still as her makeup artist was applying lashes for her. The memories of how she met Thomas Frank Porter began to come back vividly to her. The two of them met online which, at the time, was probably not the smartest thing. In the back of her mind, Mara was worried about stranger danger but enjoyed their conversations so much so that one day they both decided to meet.

At the time, Thomas had a car, but it was not running. So, Naomi decided to pick him up, but just in case he was crazy, she placed a bat in the trunk of the car. Naomi giggled to herself, thinking about how she would even try to get that bat had she found out Thomas was crazy. The day she picked him up for their date, she remembered him coming out of the apartment complex, looking very sexy to her. Thomas had on some dark denim jeans, with cute sneakers, and a white tank top on with his t-shirt in his hand. Taking a deep breath, she was relieved to see that he looked like his profile photo as she watched him walking over toward her.

Later, Thomas told Naomi that he was so nervous for their first date that he could not figure out what he wanted to wear when she arrived. She quickly noticed the sun shining on his muscles because Thomas told her many times before that he loved going to the gym. He was there at a minimum of five days a week, if not more.

While walking toward the car, Thomas pulled his shirt over his head and opened the door for Naomi to get out. They hugged and got into the car to head out to the local coffee shop. At the coffee shop, Thomas and Naomi talked for hours. That day it seemed like time slowed down and felt like they were the only two people sitting there.

Thomas revealed his love for travel, where he grew up, his journey from another country, and so much more. Each word intrigued Naomi because she longed to travel more, especially after having the opportunity to travel to places like Japan and Canada. She wanted to see the rest of the world, and Thomas seemed like just the man she could do it with. Her mind began to wonder about all the future trips they would take.

Just as quickly as she began daydreaming, Naomi was interrupted when she heard Thomas say, "I have been talking about myself, but I wanted to know more about you! What are your plans for the future?"

Naomi was not sure how to answer because she never thought about it but began to mention that "she wanted to finish up school, start her own business and travel."

Watching Thomas's face for his reaction, Naomi was pleasantly surprised when she saw his face light up with a smile as she shared with him her dreams. She could not believe a guy would sit in front of her listening to what she wanted to do or even cared about who she wanted to be. Thomas was so different. He did not even seem interested in having sex with her like countless men before but wanted to get to know Naomi.

Damn, this is so refreshing.

For Naomi, there was this oddly intimate connection with Thomas. Almost as if they had known each other from another space or time. Realizing they had been sitting there until evening, Thomas suggested that the night did not have to end there.

What could this man possibly mean by that.

Naomi found herself curious about what his thoughts were.

"Let's go see a movie," Thomas continued.

"Sure," Naomi said.

Gathering their things and heading to the car, Thomas walked around to open her door, ran around to the other side, and got into the passenger side. On the way, as she was driving, Thomas naturally placed his hand on top of Naomi's to hold it. His fingers sent a tingle through her fingertips, up her hand making its way through her whole body. There was something about him that made her feel some kind of way.

Oh, how she liked it! She loved it when he smiled, and his face seemed to light up. She liked the confidence of who he was and what he wanted. As they sat under the dim lighting of the movie theater, Thomas wrapped his arm around her. Naomi felt safe and protected, which was strange, especially since she had never met Thomas before, but he had qualities that she desired. Secretly not wanting the night to not end, Naomi pulled up to his apartment complex and let him out.

"Do you want to come up?" asked Thomas.

"Sure," said Naomi as she parked the car and followed him up to the apartment where he stayed.

The sexual tension had been building up between them both the whole evening, but now they were both ready to explode. Kissing wildly and passionately, they both found themselves tangled up in each other's bodies exploring the depths of their sexual energies. It was not until both were satisfied that Naomi grabbed her phone and saw how late it was.

"I've got to go," said Naomi hastily as she quickly got dressed.

"Well, let me walk you to your car," replied Thomas as he threw on some clothes, grabbed his keys, and walked with Naomi out to where she had parked earlier.

"Please call me in the morning when you wake up," requested Thomas, who wanted to make sure he did not scare her off or at least find out why she left so quickly.

"Yes, I will," replied Naomi as she rolled down the window, turned on the radio, and sped away.

I can't believe I had sex with him on the first night.

See, it was Mara coming back out to play again.

Dang!

Usually afterward, I never see or hear from the guy again but not Thomas.

He told me I was going to be his wife, and I laughed at him but look at where I am right now.

Realizing the makeup artist was handing her a mirror, Naomi looked into it and tried hard not to cry. She felt beautiful and amazing as she looked at the woman staring back at her. As everyone finished getting dressed, Lily helped Naomi zip up her dress and double-checked that everything looked great.

"What time is it?" Naomi asked, starting to fill up with nervous energy.

"It is almost time for us to all get into position," said

Lily loud enough for not only Naomi to hear but the bridesmaids as well.

Walking around to the front of the church, everyone started to take their place. Holding on tight to her father, Edward's arm, Naomi took one more deep breath. Waiting for the procession to file in down the aisle, she continued to take deep breaths. When the music for her turn to walk began to play, Edward and Naomi began to move forward. Finally, deciding to look up, she saw Thomas's face and saw that as she got closer to him that he shed a tear, which made her want to cry.

For them, it was not a comfortable journey to get to this moment. They had to grow pass wanting to run when things got hard, learn to communicate with each other, understand how to coexist, and so much more. Naomi knew the learning process was not over for either of them but really wanted to go on the adventure with Thomas. She saw something in him and that they could build a life together. Even though those around them were fearful and even skeptical, Naomi was convinced that their relationship was something worth pursuing. Making it down to the altar of the church, Thomas lifted her veil. Looking into her eyes, he mouthed the words "I love you" to her as she placed her hands in his.

For the whole ceremony, it felt like there was no one there other than the two of them and God. Once they got to the part where the pastor said, "Now, you may kiss the bride!" Naomi and Thomas were excited to share a passionate kiss with one another. Holding hands, they walked back up the aisle headed to the outside of the church.

Wow, we did it!

Thomas and I are now husband and wife.

I can't believe I am now Mrs. Naomi Mara Porter.

Heading into their older model Rolls Royce, their driver asked them if it was alright to drive them around for a while so the guest could make it to reception before they did. Agreeing, Thomas and Naomi held hands as they enjoyed the sights of the city.

"Thomas, thank you for choosing me to be your wife," said Naomi looking deeply into Thomas' eyes.

Filled with such a grateful heart, Naomi could not believe deep down that anyone really wanted to make her their wife. Her previous lifestyle of one-night stands or love them and leave them provided a toxic stew of mental emotions containing self-hate and rejection that caused a wake of destruction in its path.

As the driver pulled into the parking lot where the reception was being held, they exited the vehicle and lined up with the wedding party so the DJ could announce who everyone was. Walking in two by two, the wedding party entered the reception and onto the dance floor, as the DJ finally announced the newly married couple. Thomas and Naomi danced their way through the crowd and onto the dance floor.

"Let's have fun tonight," whispered Thomas in

Naomi's ear as he held her close on the dance floor, and that is what they did.

Spending the next morning recovering from their wedding night, Thomas and Naomi were excited to just lay around in bed all day. The festivities from the previous day were fresh in their minds. Now officially as husband and wife, they were happy to partake in consummating their marriage repeatedly. Rolling over, Thomas looked lovingly at Naomi while she slept. Gently placing his arm around her, he moved his body closer to hers as he lightly began to kiss the back of her neck. Opening her eyes, Naomi turned over to look Thomas in the face.

"Good Morning, my husband," she said as the warmest smile spread across her face.

"Good Morning, my wife," Thomas replied, echoing back her sentiments.

Gazing into her eyes, Thomas gathered her in his arms and softly pulled her closer to him. Kissing her lips led to a moment of passion for both, but something began to feel different this time around for Naomi. There was something deep down within her that wanted to escape from within. Unsure of what this was, Naomi tried hard to suppress the feelings that were building up and just enjoy the pleasurable moment with her husband. Unable to hold it back any longer, she felt a tear fall from her face.

I am not going to ruin this moment by crying.
Why am I even emotional?

What is happening to me?

As the tears streamed down her face, Naomi could not contain the overwhelming emotions that needed to pour out from within her. Enjoying every minute of pleasure, Thomas barely noticed the soft whimpers of crying coming from Naomi.

"That was amazing," said Thomas as he laid back down on their bed, looking up at the ceiling.

Finally, looking over at Naomi, he saw she had turned her back to him and was curled up, holding her legs.

"Hey, what is wrong?" Thomas asked.

"Nothing," said Naomi while attempting to stop the sounds of her crying.

"Naomi, something is wrong. Are you crying? Did I hurt you?" asked Thomas as a look of desperate concern now clothed his face.

"No, you didn't hurt me. To be quite honest, I don't know what happened," replied Naomi as she chose her words carefully.

Unsure of how to adequately explain what just happened, Naomi could not find the words.

"Please tell me, Naomi? What made you cry? You never cried before, so why now?" asked Thomas, who now wanted to know if he was the cause of those tears and how to solve whatever seemed to be the problem.

"I truly don't know, Thomas. I am so confused as to why I am crying. All I know, I was just overwhelmed with such deep sadness, and the next thing I know, I began crying," answered Naomi trying her best to explain.

"Naomi, I am going to ask you something you may not want to hear or even be asked, but I feel led. Have you ever been molested, raped, or touched inappropriately before? I know we have never discussed this until now. I need you to be vulnerable with me," asked Thomas as he searched Naomi's face to see what her reaction was going to be to his question.

Taking in a deep breath, Naomi began to search her mind for all the memories she had suppressed over the years so she could recall any of the missing pieces.

"I don't believe I was ever raped or molested. Now there was a time in my life when I was five years old that something traumatic happened, and from then on, I have had issues with memory recall. I often struggle to remember events. I was touched by a boy named Miguel when I was younger...I liked him and thought it was what we were supposed to be doing even though I felt bad afterward," replied Naomi struggling to find the answer to his question.

Thomas could tell that this conversation was making her feel uncomfortable. Since he was not quite sure how to help her solve the problem, he began to feel uncomfortable too.

"Alright, I am glad to hear that I did not hurt you, but you may need to talk with someone about this more, ok?" mentioned Thomas with hopes that Naomi would think about taking his advice.

Dancing with The Devil

W hen they first were married, Mara was excited to learn how to be a good wife to Thomas. That desire became overshadowed by his trust issues with her over money, his fits of rage, which occurred when he was really drunk, and his frustrating reminders of establishing his male dominance through leading by ordering. Not knowing how to address their newfound differences, Mara retreated to a space of isolation and silence. As their problems persisted, Mara, although present, felt the distance between them growing.

With the gap widening between them, Naomi got into her car, started it up, and headed out to the local coffee shop to clear her head. Arriving in her dark blue dress with her wedge sandals, Naomi stepped out of her car and was met with an intrigue of stares. Stepping into the line, she studied the menu looking for something with caramel in it. Making her way up to the counter, she placed her order and reached into her wallet to pay.

"No charge," said the barista behind the counter.

"Huh?" Naomi replied with a strange look of confusion on her face.

"The gentleman paid for your drink," said the barista pointing to a man seated at a table in the corner.

Waiting at the pickup area, Mara wondered why the guy did that. "Naomi," the barista called out as she made her way to the front to pick up her coffee. Turning around to see if the guy was still there, Mara made her way over to his table.

"Thank you for the coffee," she said as the man shifted his gaze from his laptop to face her.

"You're welcome," he answered in a deeply soulful voice.

Looking him over, Naomi saw his dreadlocks were neatly groomed and pulled back, allowing view of his muscles that bulged slightly through his white dress shirt and dark blue dress pants. His mocha skin and dark brown eyes were mesmerizing to Naomi.

Oh my!

Who is this sexy looking man?

I better leave now and head back home.

"Would you like to join me?" he offered as he got up to pull out a chair for her to sit down.

"Sure," she said as she sat down without paying any attention to her thoughts, which warned her to leave.

Extending his hand to shake hers, he said, "Where are my manners. My name is Edmund Cain."

Intrigued by his looks and politeness, she replied, "Hi. My name is Naomi Porter."

"So, I know you are probably wondering why this handsome stranger bought your coffee, right?" asked Edmund with such confidence and a sly grin on his face.

"Yes," replied Naomi, feeling drawn into his charm.

"Well, the short honest answer is I saw you standing behind me in line, could not come up with a clever opening line to introduce myself, so this was the next best thing," confessed Edmund.

"Well, I guess that was one way to introduce yourself," giggled Naomi as she realized she walked right into his plan.

"I am sorry, but I had to try something. So, what brings you here today?" asked Edmund wanting to know more about Naomi.

"I needed to clear my head, so I thought a cup of coffee and some jazz instrumentals would do the trick. What about you?" answered Naomi while studying Edmund's body language as she spoke.

"I came here to do some work before heading home but am interested in finding out more about you," answered Edmund hoping Naomi would stay a minute and entertain a conversation with him.

Sitting there for a few hours, Naomi glanced at her phone and saw a text from Thomas. It read, "Babe, where are you? I hope everything is alright. Please call me," staring off into the distance, Naomi began to feel a mixture of emotions.

Sensing the shift in her thoughts, Edmund said, "I am getting ready to finish up my work. If you don't mind talking again, take down my number. Use it if you want to or not. No pressure."

Handing her his business card, he flipped it over and wrote a set of numbers on the back.

"This is my cell, and it was a pleasure to meet you," Edmund said as he handed his card over to Naomi with a smile.

"You too," said Naomi as she stood up to leave. Walking out to the car, Naomi started it, and on the drive home could not think about anyone other than Edmund. Realizing she had not even responded to Thomas; she dialed his number. The phone continued to ring until his voicemail picked up. Naomi decided to leave a message saying, "Hey, love!" It is me. I went out for coffee but am headed back right now to the house. See you soon." Then she hit the button to hang up the call.

With nearly ten minutes more of driving until Naomi arrived home, she continued to think about Edmund. It was something about his confident charm that intrigued her. In their three-hour conversation, she found out some exciting things about him. Pulling up into her driveway and pressing the button to open the garage, Naomi pulled into the garage. Debating if she would call Edmund, Naomi entered his contact information into her phone from his business card.

Parking the car, Naomi headed through the garage door into the hallway, which led to the kitchen. Not quite sure if Thomas was home or not, Naomi headed up the stairs to their bedroom. Changing out of her dress and sandals into her cute lounging pants and top, she carefully put her purse away. Naomi grabbed her phone, and the charger then headed back down the stairs. Walking towards the living room, Naomi thought of Edmund's muscular body. Well, what she could see of it anyway.

I am married and calling Edmund for anything other than for business would be wrong, especially with me thinking about him and his body.

The sound of the garage door opening interrupted Naomi's thoughts about Edmund.

"Hey, love," Naomi said as Thomas walked up behind her and gently pulled her head back to kiss her on the forehead.

"Hey, was everything alright earlier? I texted you but got no response," asked Thomas with a sense of concern.

"I left you a voicemail, but yes, I am fine. I went out for coffee," explained Naomi.

"Well, alright. I am starving. What do we have to eat?" asked Thomas changing the subject.

"Umm... I am not sure," said Naomi as she got up from the sofa and headed into the kitchen to see what she could fix him really quick.

"I am going to get a shower and will be down in a few," said Thomas as he saw Naomi going into the kitchen to cook for him.

Finding some salmon, rice, and asparagus, Naomi began to prepare a meal for the two of them. Turning on some music while cooking, Naomi danced around the kitchen. As Thomas emerged, he noticed her mood was different. Excited to see Naomi this way, he jumped into the kitchen and began to dance and cook with her. It was these moments that brought her such joy in her marriage that it caused Edmund to fade like a distant memory.

Craving a cup of coffee on the way to work the next morning, Naomi stopped by the coffee shop and heard a familiar voice behind her while she waited in line.

"Hello, Naomi," said Edmund from behind her.

Turning around, she saw his smile and his grey suit, which fit him like a glove with his dreadlocks pulled back neatly. As Naomi stepped up to the counter, Edmund moved forward beside her and handed the barista his card to pay for her drink.

"You didn't have to do that," said Naomi as she reached into her purse to pull out the money she was going to use to pay for her coffee.

"I know I did not have to, but I wanted to," said Edmund as he started to speak his order.

"Are you stalking me?" asked Naomi as she began to feel a little strange that they ran into each other again.

"Here boss, here is your coffee," said the barista behind the counter.

"Boss?" questioned Naomi with a surprised look on her face.

"Yes. I didn't tell you before, but I am the owner of this coffee shop. I am on my way to a meeting downtown to acquire another location," replied Edmund.

So, is there anything wrong with this man?

I mean, he owns a business and is good looking.

Dang. Stop it. Don't think about this, man!

Trying to shift her focus back onto making it to work on time, Naomi smiled as she grabbed napkins for her coffee.

"Well, I hope you have a good meeting. I need to go before I am late. Thanks again for the coffee," said Naomi as she lifted up her coffee cup. Turning toward the front door, Naomi walked briskly toward her car as she could feel Edmund's eyes following her every movement. Once in her car, Naomi took a long deep sigh.

This man is truly something else.

Why did he not tell me he owned the coffee shop before.

Stop thinking about this man and get to work.

Thank goodness the office is not too far from the coffee shop.

Starting up her car, Naomi pulled out of the

parking lot and headed toward downtown. According to her navigation system, it was only about ten minutes away. Driving into the parking garage for work, Naomi located a prime parking spot. Pulling into it, she parked, grabbed her purse, and locked the car behind her. Heading toward the office, she almost ran into by her assistant Kelsey as she turned the corner.

"Good Morning, Naomi! Here is your schedule for today. First, you have a meeting this morning in the conference room that starts in ten minutes. Second, you have a property showing after lunch at 3. Lastly, did you see the fine-looking man in the grey suit with dreads?" said Kelsey excitedly.

Fine-looking man... grey suit...with dreads... it can't be.

Naomi had just recently started working in commercial real estate, and she saw many men and women in suits come through the office. Their work was more targeted toward business owners anyway, so it was not unusual. This time the description of the man sounded too familiar. Heading into her office, Naomi put down her purse and turned on her computer. Checking her email, she saw one that contained the notes for this morning's meeting. Printing off the files, she glanced through them and saw the name, Edmund.

I mean, how many Edmunds are there in the world.

It can't possibly be the one from the coffee shop.

Placing her printout into a binder along with her notebook, Naomi grabbed her phone. She made her way to the conference room. Arriving with one minute to spare, she walked in to see her broker, another male agent, and Edmund seated at the table. Trying hard not to have a shocked look on her face, Naomi tried her best to keep cool, calm and collected. Seeing her walk in, her manager interrupted and said: "Edmund, let me introduce to you our rising star and one of my finest agents, Naomi."

Turning his chair around, he looked to see who this Naomi was. Smiling, Edmund was in disbelief that this was the same Naomi he saw earlier that morning at the coffee shop. He knew now that she probably was going to think that he was stalking her. While in the meeting, Naomi and Edmund both tried to focus on what was taking place but could not fully.

I can't believe he is here at my job.

Now I know this man was not telling the truth.

He must be stalking me.

I mean of all the agencies he could have chosen; he came here.

"Naomi... Naomi. Do you have anything to add?" asked her broker looking at her with eyes that said close the deal.

"Edmund, at the end of the day the service and resources, our company can provide to help you make sound, and profitable decisions are superior to none. Now, the ball is in your court about who do you want on your team, and our company believes we don't win unless you do. Now, the only question left to ask is, do you want us on your team?" replied Naomi making a convincing argument for why Edmund should choose their agency.

Pausing for a moment to think, Edmund finally spoke up to reveal his decision.

"I want to partner with you all, but I want Naomi to run the point. I believe her insight will bring a fresh perspective to my latest investment," replied Edmund with a smile as he shook hands with her broker, the other male agent, and then her hand.

Standing up, everyone headed out of the door of the conference room to each go their separate ways. Following behind Naomi, Edmund walked up beside her.

He said: "Hey if you have a minute, I would like to discuss my thoughts and plans with you about my next business idea?"

Catching the look of let's complete this deal from her managing broker, Naomi answered, "Well, I have a moment. My office is just this way."

As they walked down the hallway to her office, Kelsey spotted them. She began wildly pointing to Edmund behind his back to let Naomi know that was the fine-looking man she was referring to earlier.

This woman right here.

I hope he does not see her.

Naomi chuckled to herself as she tried to shoo off Kelsey's apparent gestures. Entering her office, Naomi closed the door behind her and Edmund.

"So, are you going to let me in on what that was all

about back there?" asked Edmund, who saw the young woman pointing and making strange faces out of the corner of his eye.

"What do you mean? Oh, are you referring to the young lady back there that we walked past?," asked Naomi hoping that it was not that noticeable.

"Yes, I am," replied Edmund.

"I truly don't know what to say other than don't mind her," answered Naomi.

Naomi's phone on her desk rang at the perfect time.

"Hello," replied Naomi, relieved to change the subject.

"Your three o'clock appointment wants to change to a one o'clock appointment and meet you here at the office first?" said Kelsey.

Glancing at the time on her phone, Naomi saw it said 12:30 pm.

"Yes, that will work," she replied.

"Alright, I will let them know," replied Kelsey.

Turning her attention back to Edmund, Naomi saw him looking through his phone.

"Can we reschedule our meeting? I do apologize, but something has come up at the coffee shop that I need to attend to?" asked Edmund, looking up to see her response.

"Sure. How does tomorrow morning or afternoon sound?" replied Naomi.

"Well, actually, I want to move quickly on my next

project, so how about this evening at the coffee shop after closing hours?" inquired Edmund looking back down into his phone.

"Sure, that could work," answered Naomi only because the shop was not that far from her house, and she had some last-minute paperwork to do around the office.

"Perfect, I will see you at 7 pm, then?" asked Edmund.

"Yes, I will see you tonight," answered Naomi.

Standing up to leave, Edmund gently closed the door behind him. Having ten minutes to spare before her next appointment, Naomi took a moment to process what happened.

Finishing up the last of her paperwork, Naomi looked it over one more time to check it. Filing away everything, she shut down her computer, unplugged her cell phone, and grabbed her purse. Naomi had sent Kelsey home earlier and realized she was one of the last people to leave the office. Walking down the hallway, Naomi headed to the parking garage where her car was and headed to the coffee shop. Turning on the radio, she listened to some music as her thoughts from earlier that day begin to dance around in her head.

Why do I keep running into Edmund?

Why does this keep happening?

I mean earlier today at the coffee shop and then at the office.

I can't believe Kelsey called him a fine-looking man and was pointing at him like that.

Thank goodness my appointment wanted to change from three to one.

Also, I wonder what happened at the coffee shop, which caused him to leave so early.

Just as her mind was about to keep wondering on, Naomi was interrupted by a phone call from Thomas.

"Hello, love, how are you?" said Naomi, excited to hear from him.

"What do you mean, how am I? Why is there no food prepared here at home for me? I know you knew I was coming home," replied Thomas with anger building in his voice.

"I thought I had some leftovers in the fridge for you. Thomas, you know how to cook, and there is food in the fridge. Babe, I don't quite understand why this is making you upset," replied Naomi as she tried to figure out what happened to trigger such frustration in Thomas over food.

"Well, I came home and saw that the laundry you told me you were going to do was still sitting there, and now I don't have my meal prepared for me. So, Naomi, I am a little annoyed because when I ask you to do something, or you tell me you are going to do something, then I expect it to be done. So, why were you unable to get these things done," replied Thomas as he began to complain and go off on a rant.

Something must have happened earlier today for him to be taking this out on me.

I don't understand why he is so upset.

This man is treating me like his servant or maid and not his wife.

I don't mind catering to him, but what the hell is this.

I know he knows how to do the laundry and cook.

"Look, Thomas, when we met, you were cooking and knew how to do your laundry. I do not understand why today that is any different," replied Naomi agitated that she was getting talked to in this manner about something that could be easily solved.

"Well, another thing…" began Thomas as Naomi hung up the phone. She was on her way to a meeting and needed to have a clear and level head.

The fact that he wanted to argue with her over something so stupid was beginning to make her wonder what was wrong with Thomas. Turning back up her music, Naomi tried to shake off the weird fight which had just taken place.

Arriving at the coffee shop, Naomi noticed it looked closed but could see a dim light from the space right above it. She had never even looked up to notice that space before. Walking up to the front door, she saw Edmund wiping one of the tables. Knocking gently on the door, he looked up and saw Naomi; he walked over to the door, unlocked it, and let her in.

"Good Evening." Edmund said as he smiled with excitement that she even came.

"Good Evening, Edmund. I see everyone has left for the night. So, let's jump right into what you are planning for your next property," said Naomi realizing she needed to hurry up and get home to Thomas but wanted to give him space to cool off first.

"A woman who likes to get straight to business is my kind of woman," replied Edmund as he chuckled.

Sitting down at one of the tables and opening her purse, Naomi pulled out a small notepad and pen so she could take notes about what Edmund wanted to do for his next project.

"So, tell me about this next project. What are you looking to accomplish?" said Naomi, diving right into her round of questions.

"First, may I offer you something to drink? I have wine both red and white?" asked Edmund as he walked around behind the counter and pulled out two bottles from a miniature fridge.

"Why do you have wine in a coffee shop?" asked Naomi with a puzzled look on her face.

"Well, there is loft right above us, and I sometimes stay here if I am not at my other place, so the wine came from upstairs," said Edmund hoping not to scare Naomi off.

"I normally would not do this, but right now a glass of white wine sounds good right about now," answered Naomi who had planned on having a glass of wine as soon as she got home but knew she was not going to be able to enjoy it with Thomas in whatever mood that was earlier.

Pouring Naomi, a full glass of the white wine and

himself a full glass of red, he sat down in a chair next to her.

"So, for my next project... I want a coffee shop bigger than this. I would like for it to be able to have a stage area or space for one to be built. Just large enough to handle some live jazz now and then in the evenings. I want it to have the same type of branding, so, for example, the chairs and colors. I am looking at this next one possibly being in the art district area. I am open to other possible locations as well. This location has done well for me, and I am looking to open up our second, so how can I make that happen?" said Edmund as he shared his dream of opening up a second location with Naomi.

"Well, I need to know how much you are looking to profit and what you can spend on your next building location. It will help me to determine where to look and even know if there's space that can handle the things on your list that you want. I would need you to come back by the office to meet with me and have you provide me with some information for me so I can crunch some numbers," replied Naomi while taking a sip of her wine.

"Sounds good to me just let me know what you need and how soon you can set that up," replied Edmund as he took a sip of wine.

"Well, I guess that is all we can go over for right now. So, if it is not too personal of a question, please let me know what happened here at the shop earlier today when you mentioned that you needed to stop by and check on it?" inquired Naomi as she took another sip of wine.

"It is not too personal. What happened was a malfunction with one of our machines in the back, and my employees were not quite sure what to do about it. I just changed to a new mechanic that comes to work on all our machines, but I guess he could not be reached so anyway I found the number for the other mechanic and the day was saved. Now, what about you, how was your day?" asked Edmund while taking another sip.

"My day was good, just busy. I was really shocked to see you in the conference room, though. Kelsey was so funny she thought you were good looking," replied Naomi while taking another sip of her wine.

"Oh, so that was what all the pointing was about. Now I know," said Edmund as he let a deep belly laugh.

Realizing they both were down to the last sip of wine, Edmund asked if Naomi would like another one.

"Sure, but this is it. I have already drunk enough, and I need to drive home. All you have to do is climb up the stairs. By the way, where are the stairs because you sure can't see them from the front of the coffee shop or even when you are in here?" asked Naomi curious about the layout of the store.

"That is a good question. Follow me and bring your purse and wine," replied Edmund as he led her to the entrance where the stairs were cleverly hidden from view that no one would think to look.

Continuing to walk up the stairs, Edmund opened the door, which lead to this beautiful open floor plan loft, and was carefully sectioned off into different spaces. Bringing her into the living room, he helped Naomi to sit down her purse as she took another sip of her glass of wine. Turning on some jazz instrumentals, Edmund sat down next to Naomi. Starting to sway on the seat next to him, he could tell the wine was taking effect. Sliding closer, he began to place his arm gently around her. Closing her eyes, Naomi could feel the soft kiss of Edmund's lips on her neck as his hands began to move around to explore her body.

Oh my God, I should go, but damn, it feels so good.

The sexual tension which had built up from their very first encounter was now about to be acted upon through every position imagined in their heads as they moved toward the bed. Their bodies became entwined in a night of pure passion and pleasure. It was not until the sun finally broke through the windows that Naomi realized what she allowed to happen.

Damn, what have I done?

Now, I need to get home.

Dear God

Putting back on her clothes, Naomi was in disbelief at what she allowed to happen. Looking over at Edmund, she felt an instantaneous feeling of disgust for him and herself. Knowing she could not keep this from Thomas, Naomi began to wonder what he would think of her or even what he would do. As Edmund woke up, he looked over at Naomi and could see an incredible sadness in her face. Sensing that sex with him had just brought on pain more than pleasure, Edmund could feel Naomi's thoughts about him changing.

"Please forgive me, Naomi. We kept running into each other, and I could not help but think about having this moment with you. I can tell you are upset, but I am not exactly sure why?" said Edmund wondering if the reason was that it was just him or was there something else that Naomi had not shared with him.

"I apologize too. I should have never held our meeting so late or even took your offer to drink wine," said Naomi with great sadness as the weight of shame began to erupt within her.

"I hope this moment will not affect our working relationship, but understand if you feel differently," said Edmund as he got dressed and watched Naomi finished getting dressed. Helping her to make sure she had everything, Edmund led her back down the stairs to the back door exit of the loft. Walking around to the front entrance parking lot where her car sat, Naomi pressed the button on her key, pulled the handle on the car door to open it, sat down, and closed the door behind her.

Why am I so stupid!

Naomi, you could not see that Edmund wanted to have his way with your body and you with his.

All you needed was space and opportunity.

I am so damn stupid, stupid, stupid!

The drive home seemed the longest it ever had been. Naomi's mind raced nonstop, playing every possible scenario about Thomas' reaction so she could brace herself for whatever was going to happen. Pulling into the driveway and then into the garage, Naomi did not see Thomas' car. Grabbing her purse, she walked into the hallway that led into the kitchen, sat her bag on the counter, and continued walking upstairs.

I need a shower.

Also, I need to wash away everything that took place last night.

Heading straight to the master bathroom shower, Naomi turned on the water, making sure it was warm and hot. Removing her clothes and allowing them to drop to the floor, Naomi stepped into the shower. As the water flowed down over her, she began to rub her body violently as if to remove the mental and emotional stains that the other night was starting to cause her to feel.

See, you have always been a whore.

Always will be.

Even getting married could not hide the fact of who you are.

You know you enjoyed Edmund all inside of you.

So much so that you moaned several times.

Even now, you can feel everything you let him do to you.

Remember it and allow it to burn into your mind.

I will not let you forget the whore you are.

Collapsing onto the floor of the shower, Naomi could not take the presence of the overwhelming guilt and shame that assaulted her mind. She had prayed for things to get better and change, but here she was yet again. Maybe married life was not for her, and it was time to accept the role that seemed to come so naturally to her. All her life, there was never any stability in her relationships with other men. All of them were either one-night stands or a few repeat customers.

The difference between a prostitute and herself was at least a prostitute was getting paid for her services. All

Naomi had to show for this part of her life was a messy trail of tears, shame, frustration, guilt, and the attacks of depression. Getting out of the shower, she grabbed her clothes and shoved them into the bottom of the hamper, where she hoped that on wash day, she would not see them.

Heading over to her closet, Naomi found a set of her loungewear and put it on. Dreading the fact that when Thomas arrived home, she would need to confess everything to him, Naomi remembered that she had gotten some pre-rolled blunts from a contact she knew. She had started back up smoking again with Thomas even while they were married. He used it as medicine for his back pain because he believed it was helping and, in her desire, to want to spend time with him, Naomi would partake along with him.

Looking in a box that she had stashed away in her bedroom, Naomi found the weed and headed out into their backyard screened-in porch. Taking a seat on the sofa and with her lighter in hand, Mara fired up the blunt realizing that she needed a moment to think. Life over the past few years at the Porter household had become a merry-go-round of confusion and dysfunction. Between the people coming over to just hang out or socialize many times during the week, to Thomas spending time playing cards with neighbors who were only women, to moving women into their home because Thomas believed it was their job to help them and so much more.

Mara was over it. She was starting to realize that she had been on this merry-go-round long enough, and it was getting to the point where she needed to get off. The responsibility or maybe even the pressure of being married, owning and maintaining a home, working, and sometimes coming home to an empty house was just too much for them to handle at one time. Earlier on in their marriage, Mara found herself quite often alone, just trying to hold down, maintaining their home, going to school, and working odd jobs.

Mara had looked for jobs but continuously was turned down that she decided to look for work with apartments. For a season, she did not do too bad with those, but one-day was asked if she had considered working in commercial real estate. That was the day that ended up changing her life forever and led to working with her current agency.

Lighting the blunt in her hand, she gently sucked on it and held the smoke in her mouth. Finally, releasing the smoke slowly out of her mouth, she inhaled it back into her nose. Then allowed it to flow out her mouth once again.

I can't believe my life has come to this.

I thought we were stepping into a new life and opportunity to reinvent ourselves, do and be better, but here we are.

Taking another hit on the blunt as Mara's thoughts just continued to float around in her mind.

What should I do?

I don't even really know how to fix the things in my life that are broken, including me.

So, where would I even start?

What is the real reason behind why I slept with Edmund?

It must be more than I thought he was handsome or that the thought had crossed my mind.

I need to find out why I acted on it.

These thoughts were not just spurred of the moment, Mara had been thinking about these things for a while but finally realizing just how bad things were. It was as if she had walked in a daze or fog for the longest time but was not even sure how to escape.

Taking a few more hits of her blunt, Mara continued to sit there on the sofa in the enclosed porch, just staring off into the distance. Now, the effects of the weed were creeping into her body. For her, it always made her feel and desire to express her innermost sensual thoughts. Just as liquor gives some people liquid courage to do and say things they may not typically, this is what smoking did for Mara. Not only did it relax her, but she believed it helped her to show another side of herself.

Looking down at blunt in her hand, Mara realized she was about halfway through it and could tell her mental state was changing. It was an indicator for her to stop and not try to push past this limit. Even though she had tried to test her limits and boundaries before, today was not the day. Continuing to think about solutions and not just problems, Mara began to feel overwhelmed at how to explain to Thomas or even make a decision about what moving forward even looked like for herself or them.

"If you don't stop this, life will get worse," said a voice that sounded clear as the day is day and night is night.

A little startled, Mara looked around to see if there was anybody with her. Looking down at the blunt, she knew this was probably a good time to stop smoking and go back inside of the house. It was at that very moment that she heard the voice again sharing its same warning. This time Mara realized that it was God trying to tell her things have got to change.

"So, how am I supposed to do that? Said Mara in a loud, frustrated voice.

"I know that it is one thing to talk about change but another to get up and do it finally. So, how am I supposed to do that?" said Mara, shouting.

Feeling the tears beginning to well up in her eyes, Mara took one last quick hit of the blunt then put it out in her ashtray. Opening the door which led back into the house, Mara walked into the kitchen, pulled on the handle of the fridge, and got herself something with liquor in it to drink. Taking a seat on the living room sofa, Mara continued to think about what just happened and how she was supposed to change her life.

Her life with Thomas had gotten to a point where she was tired of their lack of communication, and there was never any new growth or revelation about how to become better. Mara felt like she was being held hostage on a merry-go-round as she and Thomas went through the same cycle. With all the time they invested in their relationship and purchasing a home together, Mara could not believe their lives were not built on a good solid foundation.

Even if Thomas wanted to leave me, where would I go?

How would I even start over?

If I stay, what would I need to change for things to get better?

What do I do about Edmund and this project?

Dang, I was looking forward to getting a commission check. I need to pass off this assignment to someone else.

As each question and thought began to pour into Mara's head, she began to feel the weight of an emotional heaviness within her starting to form. Not knowing the answers to these questions was where Mara's frustrations with her emotions developed. Trying hard not to spend time overthinking, Mara finished her drink and laid down to rest.

Hearing the garage door pull up, Naomi woke up with what felt like a knot beginning to form in the pit of her stomach. The moment of truth was finally arriving, where she would need to reveal her dirty secret to Thomas as the battle in her mind raged on.

You don't need to tell him.

Just say nothing and go on with your day as usual.

Only you will know.

Recognizing this voice as the side of her that

wanted to keep her from doing the right thing, Naomi closed her eyes. She began to remind herself that it would not be the right thing to do. Hearing her phone notification bell ding, Naomi looked at her phone to see a text message from her cousin Diana. Diana and Naomi were not really close but kept in touch with each other occasionally.

Opening up the text message, she saw written, "God has big plans for you but can't partner with you to make them happen if you continue to live the way you have been. Today, he wants your life to change for the better. Take a moment and ask him to come into your life. Clean up every area that has been blocking you from receiving all the wonderful and amazing things He has desired to do for and with you."

As the streams of tears began to flow, Naomi started to feel a strange sense of peace and joy, which was something she had not felt in a long time. Knowing that she needed to pray at that moment, Naomi dived right into it.

God, please help me.

Clean me up from the inside out.

I want better, but I am not sure where to begin.

Forgive me for sleeping with Edmund, and if I must reveal this to Thomas, give me courage and strength.

Amen.

Naomi never felt like her prayers with God needed to be long or drawn out. For her, the purpose of prayer was to at least be effective, even if all she could muster to say was Jesus help, or forgive me. *Diana's text was right on time. I have not prayed in forever.* As Thomas walked in, he kissed her on the forehead like he usually would then sat down on the sofa facing Naomi.

"I was debating whether to step foot in this house or not but decided to, and we need to talk, Naomi," said Thomas in such a calculated stern voice.

"Alright, I agree. We need to talk," answered Naomi sitting up straight and looking into Thomas' eyes.

"So, the other day, when I was acting out of character, I want to first apologize for my behavior. I should not have spoken to you about the food or laundry in the way I addressed it. Second, I stopped across the street from the coffee shop the other day and saw your car parked there. It was after hours, and I saw you sitting with another man. I thought about going in, but something would not allow me to. I stood for a few minutes, hoping and praying that it was nothing. I need you to be honest with me. Please tell me what was going on," said Thomas as everything he wanted to say began to pour out of him like water escaping from a faucet.

Dang, he was across the street the other night.

Now, I must confess.

Debating whether to tell Thomas the truth or not, Naomi's thoughts began to remind her of the text she received earlier. Taking a deep breath, Naomi began to gather her thoughts and just allow everything that needed to be revealed.

"Yes, I was at the coffee shop the other night with Edmund. He is a new client of mine, but little did I know that about three days prior. See, three days before that, I went to the coffee shop to clear my head when we were having an issue. I got there, and Edmund paid for my coffee, which I thanked him for, and we ended up talking for about three hours. I left and came straight home. I then saw him yesterday morning when I stopped in to get a quick cup of coffee and head straight to work. He rebought my coffee and revealed that he was the owner of the shop. He told me he had a meeting downtown about his new project. I got to the office and found out his meeting was with my business partners and me. He asked to speak with me about his project at the office after the meeting, then something came up, and he wondered if it could be at the coffee shop. So, probably when you saw me, I was sitting there going over the plans for his next shop. I was asking him for details and telling him he would need to get me budgets and other paperwork so I could crunch some numbers," said Naomi as she saw Thomas' face displaying the shock and disbelief.

Feeling that this story was not finished, Thomas asked: "Is there anything else that you need to tell me?"

"Yes, but I don't know how you are going to react or what will happen when I do," said Naomi trying to warn Thomas to brace himself.

The silence oozing from him was enough to let her know that this next part was going to be rough, but

Naomi hoped her prayer was enough to help her do what she needed to do.

Taking another deep breath, Naomi continued talking. "So, Edmund offered me wine, which I should have never taken when working with a client, but I did. See, we were arguing over food and laundry, which seemed so stupid to me. I could not for the life of me figure out what even possessed you to get all angry with me over something that seemed so easy to fix. Anyway, Edmund told me that there was a loft upstairs, and I was curious to see it. He led me up the steps with the second glass of wine in his hands for both of us. Once up there, we talked more about the layout of his next space, but then one thing led to another as we had sex. I woke up fearful realizing what happened and came straight home," said Naomi as the words came out of her mouth.

Thomas's face began to morph into one filled with disgust as he was envisioning another man doing things to his wife. Standing up, he began to pace around the room as his heartbeat began to increase. Thomas' thoughts were wildly racing to figure out what were his options right now, and he thought of everything from locating Edmund so he could beat his ass to desiring to choke out Naomi. Since both scenarios could land him in jail, Thomas continued to battle within his mind on how he wanted to handle this situation.

Seeing that he was not in his right mind, Naomi became scared to move and desired not upset him any further. All she could do was say the words help me Jesus, in her head. Noticing his pacing begin to slow down, eventually coming back to himself, Thomas sat back down on the sofa to face Naomi. Staring deep into her eyes, he began to speak.

"How could you do that to me, to us?" said Thomas, frustrated by the hurt he felt in his heart.

"I don't know what to say that will change anything," replied Mara, desperately hoping Thomas would sense or feel the sincerity from within her.

"Well, I don't know where we can go from here. I am so deeply hurt right now and quite frankly a little blinded by rage. All I know is things have got to change," said Thomas in a low stern voice.

Oh no, what could he possibly be thinking?

Quietly heading up the stairs, Thomas disappeared for what seemed like hours. Naomi could hear the rustling sound of movement, but she dared not follow him. Emerging finally from upstairs, Thomas had packed a medium-sized suitcase and headed for his car.

"Listen, I need to clear my head. I don't know when I will be back, and I would advise you not to call me," said Thomas as he disappeared into the garage and left.

Holding her head in her hands, Naomi did not know what the fate of their marriage would be but knew that she had helped to cause its demise.

See, look at what you did.

You are a whore dressed as a wife.

Look at how he just walked out on you.

Things are no different from any of the other men from before.

Overwhelmed by the weight of the horrible words that were starting to eat away at her soul, Naomi walked back out to the porch to finish smoking the other half of weed she had left earlier. Taking in each deep breath of smoke, Naomi had resolved that if she got so high that the pain would not hurt as bad, then it would be fine with her. Naomi did not want to worry anymore and just forget about what happened for a little while.

Grabbing the blanket on the sofa, she wrapped herself up and scrolled through her phone. Seeing her phone light up to reveal a text message from Edmund that read, "Last night was good, and I would love to see you again." As Naomi finished reading, she could feel a sense of anger began to rise within her but knew that she had not told Edmund that she was married because it was just supposed to be a working relationship and nothing more.

You knew better than to accept wine from a man when you have a business meeting.

Also, it was just the two of you.

Do you know he could have forced himself on you?

Do you understand the danger that you really could have put yourself through?

Not knowing how to respond to Edmund's text message, Naomi decided just to ignore her phone and gather her thoughts. Finishing up the last of her weed, she inhaled in the smoke holding it in for a long time and blew it out to consume every amount she possibly could. The uncertainty of tomorrow brought her to tears as the weed reminded her of the sensual side within. It began to tell her that she would be nothing more than this, and it was going to be her toxic cycle to carry with her for the rest of her life.

Heading back inside to the kitchen, Naomi grabbed the rest of the bottle of wine she started drinking earlier. Stumbling up the stairs, she grabbed onto the railing and headed into the master bedroom. Grabbing her phone, Naomi turned on some R&B music then cast it to her television. Dancing seductively around the room, she began to strip and dance for only herself and figured she might as well start practicing for the life that her mind told her was hers to claim. As Naomi listened to the music, the melodic rhythm and beats made her hips sway from side to side.

The desires of her flesh began to rise above all her other thoughts overpowering them on every front. Allowing herself to be controlled by these new desires, Naomi laid upon the bed and made love to herself. Making her way to heights of her climax, she screamed and curled up into a fetal position. She had experienced times of self-pleasure before, but this was different. Holding tight to her knees, the weight of the feelings of guilt, shame, and embarrassment crashed over her like a massive storm that all Naomi could do was cry herself to sleep.

Waking up the next morning to the birds chirping, Naomi felt as if a ton of bricks were being dropped on her head. Realizing she needed to head into the office, she looked at her phone to find the time and saw that it was dead.

I should have charged my phone last night.

I don't know what I was thinking.

Grabbing her tablet, she turned it on to see if she had any appointments today. Pulling up her calendar, she saw that it looked empty.

As soon as I have some charge on my phone, I will call and let someone know I am not coming in today but will be in the office tomorrow.

I will email Kelsey as well.

Quickly composing a message for Kelsey, Naomi looked it over to see if the words were spelled correctly or were just a discombobulated mess like how she was feeling now. Seeing that it looked fine, she sent it and laid back down so that the room would not feel like it was spinning. Closing her eyes, she replayed the events from last night in her mind repeatedly. She knew it could have been worse.

Thomas looked so angry the night before that it frightened her to imagine the thoughts he was thinking. It was as if something snapped inside of him, and she did not know if her prayer helped calm him down or what. Checking on her phone, Naomi saw that she had enough battery to make a call while it sat on the charger. Dialing her managing brokers' office, it rang but ended up going to voicemail. Leaving a message, Naomi explained that she would work from home but would be out of the office today. As she began to hang up, a flash of Edmund's face popped into her head.

What am I supposed to do about his account?

I need to hand it off to someone else.

I will call the other agent that was in the room with us at the time of the conference. Dialing the number of the other agent, she waited in anticipation of how this conversation was going to go then heard his voice on the other end.

"Hello, this is Scott," said the agent.

"Hi, Scott. It's Naomi. I need to hand over an account to you if you can take it," said Naomi.

"That depends which one you're trying to give me," replied Scott.

"I need you to take Edmund's account, the coffee shop owner. I have a conflict of interest and believe you can handle it more objectively," said Naomi with a sense of urgency in her voice.

"Alright, then I can take it off your hands. What do you want in return?" asked Scott, who was always thinking like an agent. "Just a referral fee of 3% for my time and energy I have already put into getting started. I can send you my notes if you want from my initial meeting," said Naomi.

"That works for me. This is not normally like you, Naomi. I figure you would have wanted to keep this one. Don't know what happened and don't care. Just know that I will take on the account and will pay the referral fee of 3%. I will talk with you later," said Scott.

"Alright, bye," said Naomi as she hung up the phone.

Turning back over, she laid back down in bed, kicking herself for having to settle for less than what she knew she could have made on this transaction. Plus, Edmund seemed like the long-term client who had plans to expand and expand.

Dang opening my legs just messed with my money, and don't get me started on my marriage if I still have one.

Now this crap right here, I can't have in my life.

Rolling back over, Naomi closed her eyes to get some rest so her head would stop hurting. As the hours continued to move forward, Naomi's mind continued to race. As she slept, the thoughts of losing a client and her interactions with Thomas seemed to replay like scenes from a suspenseful movie in her head. Screaming "No" during her dream to make everything stop brought on a lull of sudden silence. The images vanished. Looking around, she saw something very familiar but could not make it out. The room looked like her childhood bedroom. The twin-size bed sat in the corner away from the window with posters that hung on the wall from her favorite artists. *How did I get here?* she thought to herself.

Watching herself on the bed, Naomi saw her younger self sitting up on the bed in the darkness while hugging her legs with her head resting down on her knees. The room appeared to get lighter as a man in very bright clothes came over to her and began to comfort her. She could not hear the words he was speaking but could feel the overwhelming love that was exuding from his presence. Lifting her head, she began to wipe the tears that had been flowing as he extended his hand to her. Then he uttered these words in such a loving but commanding way, "Follow me."

The light around him was so comforting that Naomi saw her younger self begin to smile as she placed her hand into the man's hand as she watched him lead her out of her room and down the stairs of her childhood home. The front door swung open as the man continued to lead her through it. The bright light in front of them was so blinding she could barely see the tree which sat in front of the house. Suddenly, Naomi was filled with an overwhelming sense of peace as her mind slipped back into its deep sleep.

Deliverance

Gasping for air as her breath returned to her, Naomi opened her eyes to realize what was supposed to be a nap turned into sleeping in bed most of the day.

What kind of dream was that?

I have not thought about my childhood home for a long time.

What did that dream mean?

Scanning the room, she could tell that she was at home and that Thomas had not yet arrived back home. Recalling his ominous warning, she reminded herself not to call him and allow him the space he requested. Swinging her legs around so Naomi could let them dangle over the edge of the bed, Naomi felt a strange cloud of confusion come over her. Not knowing what to do at this moment or even how to move forward, she just sat there thinking.

Hearing the garage door opening both penetrated

her heart with a sense of relief and fear because she did not know what mood Thomas was in or even what to expect. Quickly making up the bed and throwing on her lounge clothes, Naomi raced down the stairs to the porch to get rid of her empty wine bottle and blunt.

As Thomas walked in, he smelled like whatever liquor he had been drinking the night before and had his hands wrapped from what looked like the local boxing gym not too far from the house. Pulling out a chair at the kitchen counter, he sat down and placed his hands on his head and held it bowed down. Entering the living room from the porch, Naomi could see him sitting there, and not knowing what to do began to tiptoe back up toward the stairs.

Sensing her presence, Thomas interrupted the silence by saying, "Naomi, come here so we can talk please."

Turning back around, Naomi walked to the kitchen counter and pulled out the chair next to him, then sat down.

"I had some time to do a lot of thinking, and to be quite honest, I almost jumped on the next flight out here today. I was frustrated with you, me, and us. I know I have not been the greatest husband and am still figuring this out. I have been unstable in my thinking, leading, and my jobs. I also know that there have been times I have expressed myself in ways that have hurt you and even at times have been very demanding. Please forgive me," said Thomas as he paused to gauge her reaction or even see if she was listening to him.

"I forgive you," said Naomi softly, unsure where all of this was going.

"Now, I thought long and hard about whether or not I should forgive you and if I should stay or just go. The decision I came up with is that I want to stay but let me be very clear if you ever step outside of our marriage again. We are through," said Thomas as he looked deep into Mara's eyes gauging to make sure she fully understood him.

"I understand," replied Mara feeling like a criminal on trial who was receiving her sentencing terms.

"Another thing, we need to do is communicate better. To do that, I think the best place for us to start is individual counseling, along with couples counseling. Also, maybe this will help each of us to identify why this may have happened," said Thomas.

"I agree to that," said Naomi feeling like she was negotiating a contract.

Silence fell over Thomas as he was going through his thoughts to see if he spoke about all the things he wanted to say. Part of him wanted to find out why Naomi did it but felt like it was too fresh of a wound to ask. For Naomi and Thomas Porter, their first few years of marriage had proven rocky at best.

Since they had met in such a non-traditional way, the two of them spent the first couple of years getting to know one another as they adjusted to a life of living together. The journey had been filled with working through different issues not adequately addressed or communicated before their marriage. Knowing that she caused Thomas so much pain, Mara already knew if he chose to stay with her, then she would need to work hard to earn his trust again.

Is it even possible for us to bounce back from this, or am I fooling myself?

Will Thomas ever truly trust me again, or will I forever have to continue to beg him for his trust?

Man, this road to recovery is not going to be easy, but I pray we both just give it a good try.

Breaking through the noise of her thoughts, Thomas asked, "Lastly, is there anything else that you need to tell me?"

Desiring to clear up the air between them, Thomas still loved Mara. He wanted to see if their relationship could be mended but needed to make sure there were no other hidden secrets just waiting to pop up out of somewhere.

"No," replied Mara quietly like a child who found themselves in trouble.

"Alright, then. I am going to get a shower and get some rest," said Thomas as he picked up his suitcase and went back up the stairs to the master bedroom.

Sitting motionless on the chair, Naomi found herself a little fearful of spending time in Thomas' presence due to being unaware of what mood she may encounter from him. Holding onto her phone, she saw a text message come through from her cousin Diana again. It said, "If you are looking for somewhere to go for counseling, let me know." Texting back, Naomi wrote, "Weird. Yes, I am. Please send me the information. Thanks in advance!" Waiting a few minutes, she saw Diana send her the address and phone number for a place called Inner Healing.

Strange that she would send me that right now, not knowing the conversation I just had with Thomas, but I am grateful.

I wonder if it is too late to call right now or should I give it a try.

Dialing the number, Naomi heard a voice on the other line pick up right about the third ring.

"Hello, thank you for calling Inner Healing! How may I assist you?" the voice said on the line.

"Hello, my name is Naomi, and I wanted to see if I can set up an appointment for a session and find out if you have any availability this week?" she asked hoping that she could come in soon.

"Yes, I do. I have one available for tomorrow at 1:33 pm. How does that sound?" said the voice over the phone.

"That works for me," replied Naomi.

"Have you been to Inner Healing before?" asked the voice on the other line.

"No, I have not," said Naomi.

"So, you will come to our office, and your session will be one hour long. We will just sit and talk about what you want. We will include God into our conversation through prayer too. Well, I look forward to speaking with you tomorrow at 1:33 pm!" said the voice on the phone.

"See you then," said Naomi as she hung up the phone.

Feeling a little nervous, she was not quite sure what to expect and wondered if this was going to help her any. Sitting down on the couch, Naomi turned on the television. She grabbed the blanket she kept in the ottoman until she fell fast asleep.

Waking up after what seemed like such a rough night of tossing and turning, Naomi reached for her phone to check the time. "8:00 am," she said to herself as she slid back down in the warmth of her covers and pulled them over her head. As time passed, Naomi's second alarm sounded in her favorite jazz tune, she picked as her alarm ringer. Pulling back the covers, she sat up in bed and stretched her arms. Picking up the phone on her nightstand, she saw the time read 10:00 am and then popped up in her notification was a reminder that said: "Appointment at Inner Healing at 1:33 pm".

Talking about wanting to be healed, and the whole was one thing, but it was another to make sure to set the appointment and show up. This time Naomi was finished running. She had gotten to a point where she realized that life had to be better than what it was. Naomi had dealt with these rollercoasters of emotions for over a decade now, and enough was enough. So, when Diana texted her to let her know that she should look into a place called Inner Healing, Naomi was finally ready. The day before her appointment, Naomi began to feel nervous as the questions started to dance in her head.

What are we going to talk about, will the person I speak to judge me, I am not a saint so maybe I should not talk about that time in my life.

Taking a deep breath, Naomi began to bring slow down her overactive mind and refocused on just letting go. She resolved within her thoughts that whatever needs to be revealed will come up because that area needs to be healed.

Swinging her legs out of bed, Naomi stood up to get her day started. Walking into the kitchen, she began to prepare breakfast and coffee. Finally finishing, Naomi made her way toward the bathroom to shower and get dressed. Doing a last-minute check, she grabbed her keys and purse and headed for the car. As she placed the key in the engine, Naomi released a deep sigh. Backing out of the driveway, she headed toward the freeway.

Then she turned on the radio to cope with the nervousness, which began to creep up again in her stomach. After pulling up into the parking lot outside of the building, Naomi found herself feeling even more nervous than before. It seemed so wrong that this time all she could think about was running far away. She could not believe she felt like this, especially when she had been to this exact location earlier in the week for a real estate function.

I can do this!

I have been waiting and praying for this moment.

So, just go in and face whatever is waiting for me on the other side.

She always had to do this when she felt uneasy or nervous. Well, that and go to the bathroom. Grabbing her purse, Naomi exited her car shut the door behind her, all while pressing the car lock button on her key fob. Walking up the building, she opened the door and made her way up the seventh floor. As the elevator door opened, the sign on the wall in front of her read Inner Healing Suite 777 with an arrow pointing to the right. As she rounded the corner of the office, Naomi's feelings of nervousness began to come back. "Maybe today is not a good day to do this," she thought while plotting her exit. Soon as she turned to start walking down the hall, the office door opened up.

"Naomi?" a voice calls out to her.

"Hi! I am Naomi," she says while quickly turning around to see who called her name.

"We spoke on the phone. I am Dr. Elizabeth Franklin, but you can call me Dr. Elizabeth. It is nice to meet you," said a woman dressed in light blue jeans with a fitted white scoop neck t-shirt while extending her hand to shake Naomi's hand.

"So, what brings you in today?", Dr. Elizabeth said as they both sat down in chairs from across each other.

"Well, I have been so tired of living the way that I have. So, I decided to see if something could be done," replied Naomi with a slight hint of hesitation in her voice.

"Well, whatever you want to share with me is what we will talk about. Now, I would like to open and close with prayer in our session, but if I hear something from the Holy Spirit, then I will reveal it to you. What is shared here in this space is confidential," stated Dr. Elizabeth before moving the conversation forward. While praying along with Dr. Elizabeth, Naomi sat there, convincing herself to see the session through to the end.

I want to run away, but I know this is where I need to be.
God help me to understand why I am here.
Please reveal to me why my life took such a wrong turn.

As the prayer ended, they both said Amen.

"Is there anything specific that you would like to talk about today, Naomi?" asked Dr. Elizabeth.

"Yes, I am here because I have shame, depression, and anger issues that happen so randomly at times. My husband Thomas and I are trying to work things out, but he has been acting really strange with me. So right now, at this very moment, I feel very unloved, unworthy, and hurt. When I gave God my yes to his will and way, it seems like all I received in return was pain and heartache. My faith has been attacked so strongly in this season of life. Quite frankly, I am tired of holding on," answered Naomi as all the pent of frustration and desperate need for answers just gushed out from within her.

As Naomi spilled out her inner thoughts, Dr. Elizabeth sat quietly, taking notes. Sometimes jotting down what Naomi may have mentioned but other times writing down other things.

"May I ask you a few questions?" Dr. Elizabeth asked.

"Yes, sure, go ahead," replied Naomi.

"Do you and your husband or ex-husband have children?" asked Dr. Elizabeth.

"No, we don't," answered Naomi.

"Also, how long have you and Thomas been separated, and do you have any plans to reconcile?" asked Dr. Elizabeth.

"At first he told me he wanted to stay but late last night mentioned that his thinking of changing his mind. We have not separated but are thinking about it. No, we don't want to get back together. He told me that he does not want to be with me anymore, and I told him that I want a divorce, too," replied Naomi beginning to feel uncomfortable by the questions.

Hearing herself speak about these things out loud made them seem so real even though they happened not that long ago.

"Thank you for answering those questions for me. At this time, Naomi, I would like to pray over things that you shared with me today?" said Dr. Elizabeth bowing down her head. Naomi prepared her heart and mind to receive the prayer that was being said over her.

"Father, God. I lift up your daughter Naomi to you today. I thank you, Father, that she came here today searching for inner healing, so we ask that you begin the process of healing her today. I come against the feelings of unworthiness, rejection, pain, frustration, rage, and anger. Please remind her today and at this very moment that you love her. Help her in this season to see you for the God that you say and declare you are. Amen," said Dr. Elizabeth.

As Naomi said "Amen," an overwhelming sense of peace came over her as tears began to fall from her eyes.

Realizing the weight of this session on Naomi, Dr. Elizabeth handed a tissue to her so she could wipe away the tears.

Wow, that was intense.

All she did was break off some things, listen, and pray.

I guess this is where I need to be.

Dr. Elizabeth interrupted her thoughts by asking if she would like a drink of water. Walking out of the room, Dr. Elizabeth went into the waiting room area and got a cup of water for Naomi. Upon returning, Dr. Elizabeth handed her the cup of water, sat down in her chair, and began to close out their session.

"So, Naomi, while you were talking, I was taking some notes, and I wanted to take a moment to share those with you. As you were talking, I saw your heart broken into these small pieces. What that means is you're experiencing a fragmented soul," said Dr. Elizabeth softly.

"A what?" replied Naomi while looking up from the tissue she placed over her face to shield the tears.

"For example, when we experience trauma, parts of our soul break off. These parts sometimes become hidden for us to deal with later or exposed for us to deal with them now. Trauma can present itself by showing up in our outward expression of our emotions, such as fear, anger, bitterness, etc. Or even as pain throughout different parts of our bodies such as the brain (more specifically our memories), the heart, or the gastrointestinal system, to name a few," explained Dr. Elizabeth.

"So, you mean to tell me that the random fits of anger, sadness, and depression I've been experiencing could be connected to my experiences of trauma?" questioned Naomi feeling puzzled by this new revelation.

"Yes!... Here at Inner Healing, we work from the inside out. Meaning we look to find out what trauma you been through and behaviors you are experiencing, then reveal it through our proven methods to bring healing and restoration to that area," clarified Dr. Elizabeth about the process.

"Naomi, I recommend that you set up weekly sessions or come in for one of our in-depth sessions. Our in-depth sessions allow us to work with you longer than what we can accomplish in 1 hour. We can work on healing on a much deeper level," continued Dr. Elizabeth while slowing down to not overwhelm Naomi with too much information.

Hesitating for a moment, Naomi was shocked by how much was revealed in only her first session.

"Let me think about it, but for now, please sign me up for another one- hour session," said Naomi after finally gathering her thoughts and words together.

"Alright! How does Friday at 2 pm sound?" asked Dr. Elizabeth.

"Sounds good. I will see you then."

Naomi said as she stood up from her chair while lifting her purse onto her shoulder.

Making her way out of the office and toward the elevator, she pressed the down button. Stepping into the elevator and pressing the lobby button, Naomi's mind began to review the session that she just had. Her thoughts began to race one after the other again.

I wonder what trauma I faced in the past.

How is it possible for old trauma to even affect me now?

If I've moved on, then I should be fine, right?

As the elevator door opened to the first floor, Naomi walked quickly to her car, opened the door while starting up the engine, and turned on the radio, hoping that it would provide a welcome distraction to the thoughts which were consuming her mind.

The drive home was filled with trying to process all that had just taken place.

I wonder if the moments with Miguel were a part of why I had random moments of anger.

This infidelity I put Thomas and I through has brought up feelings of rejection and loneliness which need to go away.

Now Dr. Elizabeth mentioned dealing with trauma, and I wonder if there are any hidden moments that I have dealt with and did not know.

I don't know what I am going to do.

Finally arriving home, Naomi realized there were many things she should have dealt with before walking down the aisle and saying I do. It never occurred to her to even try to look deep within herself before taking on the responsibility of loving someone else. It was not fair to her or Thomas. Thinking back on when they met, Naomi was in such a place of darkness and despair that she did not even consult with God if Thomas was the one for her.

Wow, I decided something so life-changing on my own.

What is scary is that I never even thought to examine his heart and motive for truly getting married to me.

Parking her car into the garage, Naomi entered into the hallway that led to the kitchen. Placing her purse down on the counter, she washed her hands at the sink and opened up the fridge to see what she could make quick for dinner. Grabbing some ingredients to make a hearty salad, Naomi began to chop away. Her mind was so preoccupied with chopping and reviewing her session that she didn't even notice Thomas come into the kitchen.

"Hey, Naomi," said Thomas wondering why she was staring off into the distance.

"Oh, hey, Thomas," she answered back, finally realizing what she was doing.

"Are you alright? You were just staring off while cutting up the food in front of you?" asked Thomas feeling a little unsettled by her doing that.

"Yes, I am fine. I just had my session today, and it was good and revealing. I don't know how to feel, and it gave me some things to work on," replied Naomi.

"Well, my session was canceled today, so I guess I am going to have to reschedule," said Thomas.

Something does not sound right.

I don't remember him asking me for the number to this place or even him telling me that he signed up for a session anywhere for that matter.

He can't possibly think I am the only one in our relationship with issues but let me slow down and find out.

"So, why did you not reschedule when you found out it was canceled?" said Naomi curious to understand his reasoning.

"No, I will call back later in the week, though. I am glad that your session was good. Maybe you can get to the bottom of why you cheated on me," said Thomas as he walked away into the living room and turned on the television.

Feeling the sting of his last comment hit her heart, Naomi tried very hard not to get offended by what he said. It was starting to seem like his sly off-color comments were becoming more like weapons to chip away at her confidence by proving she was nothing more than her mistakes. Shaking it off, Naomi continued to make the salad and decided that it may not be enough food.

Pulling out the ravioli from the pantry, she grabbed a large pot and put some water to boil. Once those were cooked, she carefully removed the water and added the sauce to it. Calling Thomas to let him know that it was time to eat, Naomi plated his food and sat it down in front of him.

"Get me a soda while you go back to get your food," said Thomas as he began eating. Following his command, she grabbed a soda from the fridge and placed it in front of him.

"Hey, I am going to eat this over by the sofa," he said as he lifted his plate and moved over to the living room.

Getting her food, Naomi sat in the kitchen by herself and tried to hold back her tears as she started to feel more alone than she ever had in years. Grabbing her phone, she began to scroll through it just to pass the time. Finishing his meal, Thomas placed his plate and soda on the counter and headed off into another room.

"Take care of this for me," said Thomas as he walked away.

Quietly Naomi got down from her chair and threw the soda can in the trash and placed the plate and fork in the sink and returned to finish her food. After finishing, Naomi walked around to the sink with her plate, fork, and cup as she grabbed the dish soap and poured it into the sponge so she could wash them. Cleaning the pots and pans, Naomi put all the leftover food in containers, wipe down the counters, swept, and finally was ready to head upstairs to get some rest. Walking into the master bedroom, she heard a noise which sounded like snoring, and there laid Thomas fast asleep. Trying hard to suppress the rage she was feeling, Naomi wandered into the guest room to lie down and fall asleep.

The day for her next session with Dr. Elizabeth had finally arrived, and Naomi was excited to learn some more new things and see how she could finally start to move toward a better life. Before walking into Dr. Elizabeth's office, Naomi prayed a quick prayer.

Have your way, God, but today, please help me learn what has been holding me back from living the abundant life that you have for me.

Opening the door, she was greeted by Dr. Elizabeth, who mentioned she was just about to wrap up with the person who was there before her. Patiently waiting, Naomi saw her phone light up with a notification saying she had a text from Thomas. It read when you come home, make sure you are ready for me. Don't play with me this time. I want all of you like you let that man have you too.

Watching as Dr. Elizabeth came back in and

signaled that they could get their session started, Naomi followed her, and they opened with prayer.

"So, what brings you in today, Naomi?" asked Dr. Elizabeth.

"Well, I am having trouble dealing with my husband Thomas right now. I recently slept with another man, and Thomas mentioned that he wanted to forgive me and work things out. Still, instead, I am getting snarky remarks and feeling like I am even more punished. I mean, I know he is hurting and right now does not trust me, but he has never treated me like this before. To be quite honest, I would rather him give me the silent treatment or even want to leave me at this point. I am so confused because the last time we saw each other, I mentioned that Thomas and I thought about separating. Also, I am here because I wanted to get to the bottom of why I have endured so much pain at the hands of other men myself. I don't understand why I struggle with lust and fornication," said Naomi, hopeful that maybe in this session, she could discover answers to the questions that began to burn deep within her from her previous session.

"Alright, let's go into the prayer and see," said Dr. Elizabeth. As she started praying, she began to ask Naomi questions, "were you ever touched inappropriately by anyone other than Miguel?"

"I don't know because I can't always remember events well from my past," replied Naomi.

"What was the relationship between your parents like?" inquired Dr. Elizabeth.

"It was good, I guess, but there was my father's

previous wife, who I believe may still carry the last name, Johnson as well," replied Naomi.

"So, today, we are going to break off from your life two things: any molestation or rape that may have occurred and illegitimacy," said Dr. Elizabeth.

"Illegitimacy? I thought that meant that you don't have your parents or something," said Naomi wondering how this may apply to her.

"Illegitimacy, in this case, can just refer to your parents being married to each other. Your father's previous wife may not have been all the way divorced from him. So, when they had you, it can open you up to spiritual warfare in areas such as perversion, lust, fornication, addiction, etc. You may even battle with feeling or calling yourself stupid, worthless, or dumb. The enemy uses this as a doorway to come into your life to attempt to steal your identity. See, your identity in Christ is who God created you to be here on earth and what you do here actually does matter. Whatever assignment you were created to do here can bring about generational blessings but like everything God gave us the ability to choose if we would do that or not?" explained Dr. Elizabeth

"I can relate to all that. I have even found myself saying I am stupid or dumb, especially when I make a mistake. It seems like, at times, I am unable to do or say the right thing. So, I can be very hard on myself because of this and have struggled with addictions to sex, liquor, and drugs. This has been my comfort or cover plus it seemed like every boy or man I encountered only saw me like a whore, so a whore I figured I would become," said Naomi.

"Well, let's pray. Dear Heavenly Father, Thank you for your beautiful daughter. Every area of pain she's experienced, please remove it and fill her back up with the fruits of your Spirit. Loose upon her, your love, joy, peace, patience, kindness, goodness, faithfulness, gentleness, and self-control, Father. Today, we bind up the spirits of addiction, perversion, lust, fornication, and illegitimacy by the power of the blood of Jesus, who laid down his life to overcome the transgressions of this world. We command every spirit to go back to the abyss from which they came into her life. We ask that you close behind them every door and ask that you seal it shut. In Jesus' name, we pray Amen," proclaimed Dr. Elizabeth.

Covering her face with her hands as the tears began to flow, feeling such a weight lifted from within her, Naomi began to feel lighter. Not understanding what was happening, she knew that her prayers were being heard.

Speechless and not sure what to do, Naomi got up and realized she finally had language for what she had gone through. Feeling a long overdue weight lifted, she knew this was the beginning of regaining her identity back. Thanking Dr. Elizabeth and grabbing her purse, Naomi headed for the door. Stepping into the hallway, she walked over to the elevator and pressed the button to go down.

As the elevator finally settled on her floor, the doors rolled open, allowing Naomi to step through. Riding

down to the first floor, she was in shock about all the revelation that was presented to her. Heading toward the glass door entrance, Naomi pushed open the door and made her way into the parking lot toward her car. Pressing the button on her key fob to unlock the door, Naomi opened it and slid into the seat. Stunned, she rolled down the windows and sat in the car, thinking to herself.

Thank you, God, for revealing the hidden things to me.

Thank you for uncovering the shame and guilt.

Thank you most of all for waiting for me.

Finally, having the focus to drive, Naomi started the car, pulled out of the parking lot, and headed home.

Letter to The Reader

Consistently, we are warned about the physical consequences of sexual sins, such as producing a baby without marriage, the high risks of contracted diseases, and the alterations to our lives, including money and time, to name a few. But we are never warned about the spiritual effects. For instance, I don't recall being told to protect myself from the demonic forces that could enter me or that sex outside of God's will (a godly ordained marriage) is like playing with Pandora's box. I never fully understood that my choices to have multiple partners would lead me to hear various voices in my head, develop mental health problems, or that I would experience becoming suicidal.

For many of us, these stories, like the one I shared with you about some parts of my life, are so taboo that no one talks about them. We are told time and time again not to speak about these things or to embarrass our family name. So, instead of getting the help we so deeply desire, we quickly turn back to the destructive things that we know can help to fill the void. When all we wanted was to be loved, and I mean genuinely loved! Please remember that there is a solution. His name is Jesus! He loves you and wants to see you healed more than you may ever fully comprehend! Then seek out an accountability group that could be in the form of a therapist, counselor, or a small group of friends that you can trust to help you through. Also, remember as you begin your journey toward healing to be kind to yourself and keep working on it one day, one minute, one second at a time!

For you are worthy of being loved!

Sincerely,
    Jacinta